Secrets of the Duke's Family

The mysteries and passions of the aristocracy!

Lady Margaret and Lady Olivia are hoping their brother, the Duke of Scofield, will sponsor a season for them. They're desperate to start their lives and to find the fairy-tale romance that awaits them in society's ballrooms.

But with rumors circulating that the duke murdered their father to get the title, scandal stalks the family wherever they turn. They must weather the storm as the truth is revealed...and as they fall, unexpectedly, irresistibly in love along the way!

Read Margaret's story in:
Lady Margaret's Mystery Gentleman

You won't want to miss the other books in Christine Merrill's Secrets of the Duke's Family trilogy

Coming soon!

Author Note

Like a lot of you, I spent a fair amount of time in 2020 hunkered down in my house, waiting for time to pass. At times like that, it is always nice to return to comforting old-favorite books and TV shows.

For me, it was Agatha Christie. While waiting for the curve to flatten, I found an endless parade of bodies in quaint English villages with Miss Marple, took multiple train trips with Hercule Poirot, and introduced my husband to Tommy and Tuppence Beresford.

When it came time to write, some of that mayhem was bound to rub off. And that is why, for the next few books, we will be trying to sort out the mysterious happenings at the town house of the Duke of Scofield. Family secrets will be uncovered! And, of course, true love will conquer all the non-murder-related problems.

CHRISTINE MERRILL

Lady Margaret's Mystery Gentleman

HARLEQUIN®
HISTORICAL™

ISBN-13: 978-1-335-50593-4

Lady Margaret's Mystery Gentleman

Copyright © 2020 by Christine Merrill

This edition published by arrangement with Harlequin Books S.A.

For questions and comments about the quality of this book,
please contact us at CustomerService@Harlequin.com.

Harlequin Enterprises ULC
22 Adelaide St. West, 40th Floor
Toronto, Ontario M5H 4E3, Canada
www.Harlequin.com

Printed in U.S.A.

Christine Merrill lives on a farm in Wisconsin with her husband, two sons and too many pets—all of whom would like her to get off the computer so they can check their email. She has worked by turns in theater costuming and as a librarian. Writing historical romance combines her love of good stories and fancy dress with her ability to stare out the window and make stuff up.

Books by Christine Merrill

Harlequin Historical

The Brooding Duke of Danforth
Snowbound Surrender
"Their Mistletoe Reunion"
Vows to Save Her Reputation

Secrets of the Duke's Family

Lady Margaret's Mystery Gentleman

Those Scandalous Stricklands

Regency Christmas Wishes
"Her Christmas Temptation"
A Kiss Away from Scandal
How Not to Marry an Earl

The Society of Wicked Gentlemen

A Convenient Bride for the Soldier

The de Bryun Sisters

The Truth About Lady Felkirk
A Ring from a Marquess

Visit the Author Profile page
at Harlequin.com for more titles.

To Jim and Sean,
for taking one for the team.

Chapter One

'You are being unfair.' Lady Margaret Bethune leaned forward, her knuckles on her brother's desk, wishing she could bully him into cooperation. When one was but five foot two and only nineteen, intimidation was a vain hope. It was even more unlikely when speaking to one of the most powerful men in the country. But she had already tried sweetness and tears and they'd got her nowhere. She was running out of ideas.

The Duke of Scofield did not even look up from his newspaper to acknowledge her display of temper. 'You might find me unfair, but it is entirely within my right to do as I think fit. I am guardian to you and your sister and make the rules for the household.'

'But your rules are unreasonable,' she replied, exasperated. 'Every other girl my age has already come out. Why are you refusing a Season to me?'

'Because it is too soon,' he said, still not looking up.

'Too soon after what?' she demanded. 'If you are referring to Father's death, that was almost two years ago. We have been fully out of mourning for some time.'

'Maybe next year,' he said with a sigh, as if the conversation fatigued him. It probably did. Peg doubted it was easy for him to see Olivia and herself as women almost grown instead of the little girls he had played with in the nursery.

'Next year, I will be almost one and twenty,' she said. 'When I come of age, I will be able to make the decision on my own.' But even then, her brother would hold the purse strings and could make her do as he pleased.

He looked up to fix her with a stern expression. 'Then I hope you will remember that you are still my youngest sister. It would be unseemly for you to be looking for marriage when Olivia is not yet matched.'

'Do not pretend that Liv wants to be a spinster,' she replied. 'She has been ready to marry for some time. Her wedding will occur the minute you are willing to accept the suit of any of the men who have offered for her.'

'When a satisfactory candidate for marriage presents himself, I will allow the fellow access,' Hugh said, giving his paper a dismissive rattle.

This was an outright lie. Olivia had had a string of suitors eager for her hand since long before Father had died and their brother had refused them all without explanation. But it would do her no good to challenge him on it. If he became angry, he would send Peg from the study and refuse to listen to her at all.

Instead, she tried to be the naive and accommodating sister that he must wish he had. 'It is good to know you are open to her marriage. But how will she meet such a man if you do not allow either of us out of the house?'

'That is an exaggeration,' he replied. 'You both went to Bond Street just yesterday.'

'Bond Street.' She sniffed, unable to contain her disdain. 'A little shopping hardly signifies when we have nowhere to wear the things we buy. You refuse the majority of the invitations that are offered to us and turned down the vouchers when the patronesses of Almack's sent them. I do not understand why you brought us to London with you if you will not allow us to socialise.'

'I brought you here so I could keep a watchful eye over you. It is my duty to do so.' At this, he looked up at her with a worried frown, as if he were sincerely concerned for her welfare. His reaction made no sense. Since nothing ever happened at Scofield Manor, they would have been safer in the country than they were when exposed to the temptations of the city.

It was clear that her argument was getting nowhere, so Peg walked to the door of the study and stuck her head into the hall, seeking reinforcements. 'Liv! Come in here and help me reason with Hugh. He thinks he must watch us every minute to keep us out of trouble. You must tell him we are better than that.'

Her sister Olivia, who had been coming down the stairs at the end of the hall, froze like a rabbit in front of a fox.

Peg gestured furiously to show her that it was too late to retreat. Then she gestured back towards the office and their brother.

Liv gave a violent shake of her head and waved her arms in silent refusal as Peg ran out to take her by the elbow and drag her into the argument.

When they arrived in front of his desk, Hugh glanced up long enough to note the other girl's presence, then went back to his paper. 'And I suppose you want another Season, as well?'

'That is not necessary, I enjoyed my first one very much,' Liv said, hurriedly, glaring at Peg for involving her in the conversation. Then, she added, 'But if you would accept the latest offer that has been made for me, it would not be an issue. I would be married already and would save you the expense of my wardrobe.'

She was referring to Alister Clement, a gentleman whom she had been sweet on for quite some time and whom their brother had taken an instant dislike to. Since Mr Clement was as unobjectionable as it was possible to be, it was more proof of how unreasonable Hugh had become.

'When an acceptable offer is made, I will agree to it,' he said, to remind her that Clement had already been rejected. 'Until then, you must trust me to know what is best for you.' He gave her a long, cold look to tell her that the matter was not open for discussion.

Liv's mouth opened and closed again, containing her argument in subservient silence.

Since she would not fight for her own future, Peg would have to do it for her. 'Without another Season, there will be no more offers for Liv,' Peg reminded him. 'And if you will not allow me to marry until she does, you must mean to keep us both spinsters for ever.'

There was a pause before he answered, as if he did not want to admit that that had been exactly what he had been intending. Then, he smiled and replied, 'Do not be melodramatic. I am sure you will both be married in good time. Just not this year. Until then, you must find other ways to fill your days that do not involve husband hunting.'

'And what are they, precisely?' Peg asked, tapping her foot in irritation.

'Until today, you never seemed to tire of shopping,' he reminded her. 'But if that has paled, you could visit London's many museums or lending libraries and make an effort to better yourselves.'

'Libraries and museums,' Liv said, nodding obediently and backing slowly towards the door. Since either of those might give her an opportunity to meet her beau in secret, she probably wanted to claim the trips before Peg angered the Duke to the point where he might forbid going out at all.

Before she could escape, Peg clutched her arm

and pulled her back to the desk. 'Frankly, we cannot imagine anything more dull.'

'We?' said Liv in a weak voice, shaking her head to distance herself from the statement.

The Duke's face darkened. 'Then perhaps a return to finishing school is in order, for one of you, at least.'

At this, Peg laughed. 'I am old enough to be fully finished by now. I doubt more education will help me.'

Her brother gave an exasperated huff. 'Then perhaps you could practise the skills you already have. The pianoforte, watercolour...'

'We have done both of those until our fingers ache,' Peg said in disgust. Next, he would be suggesting good works and fervent prayer, neither of which would get her any closer to the Season she longed for.

Other girls her age were dancing and flirting, having the sort of tame romantic adventures they could exaggerate when writing in their diaries and gossiping with their friends. Not only had Peg not been kissed, she had only her sister to complain about it to.

What could she say to sway Hugh to leniency?

She bit her lip to prevent another outburst and considered her next move. She must give him a suggestion that made accepting the next invitation to a rout or a ball seem like the safer option. She smiled as she thought of something so outrageous that she was sure he would rather see them at Almack's than to accept. 'We are quite proficient in all the ladylike arts you have suggested. But there is one area of education that we have sorely neglected.'

'And what is that?' he said, throwing his hands in the air. 'If it will get you to stop pestering me for vouchers, I will consider it.'

'You could hire us a dancing master,' she said. 'Since we have not been going about to balls, we do not know the latest steps and have fallen out of practice with the old ones. If you could hire a gentleman to come here and teach us in private, we will be able to dance without leaving the house. With a little instruction we will be ready to return to society when you are ready to allow it.'

'Dancing lessons,' he said, his mouth tightening in disapproval at the suggestion.

Good, she thought. Perhaps now he would see that it was better to leave the house than to allow risks over the threshold.

If he was serious about protecting them, he would never agree to leave his two sisters home alone in the company of a strange man while he was in his seat in the House of Lords. Since they went out so rarely, he had not bothered to engage a chaperon to watch over them. Two bored girls and private lessons involving physical contact with the opposite gender was a situation ripe with temptation.

Even she found the idea rather shocking. But if she wanted him to take her seriously, Peg must pretend that the risks had not occurred to her. She gave him her most vacuous smile and added, 'It will be almost as good as going to an actual ball. And I am sure we will learn so many things we did not know before. You do not want us to be socially stunted, do you?' She waited for his explosion.

'Socially stunted?' Instead of anger, she thought she saw his mouth quirk towards a sceptical smile, before returning to its usual, impassive position.

She responded with wide-eyed sincerity, 'We are the sisters of the Duke of Scofield. We must prepare to be at ease in any situation. But now we are woefully out of touch.'

In the silence that followed, she imagined she could hear the mechanical clicking as the cogs in his brain turned, weighed the possible risks of her suggestion and tried to find a better alternative. Then he sighed, his face relaxing in a satisfied smile. 'Very well. I will advertise for a dancing master. And if you are having any girlish fantasies of me allowing some handsome rogue into the house, you had best quash them now. I mean to hire the oldest and ugliest one I can find. I will expect a demonstration of the skills you have learned in one month's time. If you are not proficient by then, I will call an end to the whole fiasco and we will go back to things as they were.'

Perhaps she should have left it to Liv to find a way around their brother for this was not the response she had expected at all. Dancing around the drawing room with a stranger would not get her a single step closer to Almack's. Even more infuriating, Hugh was now staring at her as if he expected thanks.

She gave him a gritted smile in return and replied, 'We will not disappoint you. I promise.'

He sighed as if they already had. 'I am glad we have come to an understanding. Do not worry your pretty heads about the matter. Go back to your day and I will see to everything.' He made a vague shooing motion with his hands to send them from his office.

'He cannot be allowed to get away with his crimes.' In the office of the *Daily Standard*, David Castell paced the floor in front of his editor's desk, his fists balled as if ready to settle the matter in the way he truly wished to, *mano a mano.*

'But he has and he will,' Mr Jakes replied with none of the pent-up emotion being displayed before him. 'Nothing is ever done when members of the peerage overstep the bounds of legality since they are left to police their own indiscretions. Scofield is a duke. That is as close to being above the law as one can be.'

'But this is not a matter of a few bad debts or illegal duels. This is murder.'

'Two murders,' Jakes said in the same dry tone. 'Neither of them proven.'

'Trust me, I have not forgotten about the old Duke of Scofield,' David said with a bitter laugh. 'It is common knowledge that his son did away with him.'

'Common knowledge,' Jakes said with a disapproving sniff. 'If I publish that without proof, he will bring suit against me for libel. And even though his fellows in the House of Lords are sure he committed murder, they did not hang him for it two years ago when it happened. What makes you think that this time will be different?'

Because it had to be. Dick Sterling had been David's friend. No man deserved to die with a knife in his back, his body dumped into the Thames like garbage. Since it was clear that the law had no interest in investigating, it was up to David to see that the killer did not walk free. 'This time it will be different because the evidence against Scofield will be presented in my article on the front page of your newspaper. No one will be able to look away or make excuses, as they have done before.'

'And just where do you mean to find this evidence?' Jakes said, leaning forward in his chair. 'Let us assume for a moment that you are right. If anyone knows the truth, they have been afraid to come forward with it. Why will they talk to you?'

David reached for the copy of the paper that was sitting on the corner of the desk, turning pages and folding them back to reveal the classified advertisements. He pointed to the one that had caught his eye. 'Scofield is searching for a dancing master, probably for his two sisters. I mean to present myself as said employee. Once I have gained entrance to the house, I will search the place and question the staff. Perhaps I can get one of the girls to reveal a detail they do not know is important. I am sure that there is someone in that house who has seen something or knows something.' It was the best place he could think to look, since the people he had interviewed outside the house had been less than forthcoming.

Jakes laughed. 'And why do you think that they will hire you?'

'To begin with, I expect there will be few candidates for the job, since you will accidentally stop running the ad after today,' David said with a smug grin. 'Then, there are the excellent references I have already procured from my own half-sisters.'

Jakes raised an eyebrow. 'You are fortunate that your family accepts a bastard son at all, much less is willing to lie for him.'

'I doubt my father would approve of their lying for me,' David said with a shrug. 'But what he does not know will not hurt him. I appealed to his daughters, who were thrilled at the chance to involve themselves in my investigation. They find it a novelty to read my articles in the paper. They also told me that there is no chance Scofield will ask my father directly about the matter, since the two do not speak. In Father's opinion, Scofield is a scoundrel who deserves whatever justice might come to him.'

Jakes eyed him thoughtfully. 'And I suppose it would be to your advantage if your father learned that you had delivered said justice.'

David shrugged. 'The thought had occurred to me.' He did not precisely want to curry favour with a man who'd had little use for him since his conception. But neither was he so foolish as to refuse the man's approval, should he finally manage to get it.

Jakes continued. 'If I agree to this, it is on the understanding that, if it fails, as it is likely to do, I never gave you permission or encouragement. I will not let your vendetta tarnish the reputation of this newspaper.'

'If it fails, which it will not, I doubt you will have to worry about your reputation,' David said with another grin. 'You are imagining he will take you to court. I think it is far more likely that if Scofield realises I am investigating him, I will be found in the same condition as my friend, floating dead in a river somewhere.'

'Then I promise your obituary will be a whole column long,' Jakes said with a smile.

'I couldn't ask for anything more than that,' David replied.

Chapter Two

It took only a day before David had the opportunity to test his plan. His answer to the advertisement was met almost immediately with a letter inviting him for an interview at the Scofield town house.

To prepare, he slicked back his hair with Macassar and put on his shiniest pantaloons and a suit coat that was so tight he could barely raise his arms. The reflection that looked back from the mirror was that of a man more concerned with his clothes than the women he taught. To complete the disguise, he affected a broad Italian accent, since it was often thought that Continentals were better dancers. More important than that, a different nationality would distance him from the current social set, should Scofield think him familiar. He doubted that the Duke would recognise him, for they seldom frequented the same places and had never been introduced. But it would be the height of foolishness to assume the peer's ignorance, simply because he wished it to be true. If

David was recognised, his investigation would be over before it started.

Now that he faced Scofield in person, he was afraid his disguise would not be enough. The Duke was looking at him as though he could see past his appearance and into his soul. Perhaps, as a man of great power, he had come to expect that others were not always as they seemed. He greeted David with a prolonged silence and another penetrating stare. The combination was probably enough to make a weaker soul confess deception before the interview had even begun.

David resisted, falling deeper into his character as one who aspired to the position of employee in a great house. He dropped his head a fraction, attempting to appear subservient and perhaps a little frightened. While he did not want to avoid the peer's gaze in a way that might seem suspicious, he was careful not to look him directly in the eye. It would be unwise to do anything that might seem like a challenge to such a man.

When it was clear that he was not going to babble hidden truths or break and run, Scofield seemed satisfied and glanced down at David's falsified references. 'These are most impressive, Mr Ricardo Castellano.'

'*Grazie,*' David said, then added a subservient nod. 'The ladies of Lord Penderghast's family were most satisfied.'

'Not too satisfied, I trust.' Scofield was staring

at him again, as if waiting for him to admit to an indiscretion.

'I do not understand,' he said with a shrug.

'I do not believe you,' the Duke replied. 'But at least you are smart enough to answer in the way you know will please me.' He looked up again and one eyebrow raised a fraction of an inch to indicate his scepticism.

'I would never…' David paused for a moment, pretending to search for the right words '…presume familiarity with my students.'

'That is wise of you,' the Duke replied in a tone that did not sound convinced. 'I was hoping to find a man who was older and less…' He gave a disgusted shake of his head.

David replied with another shrug. 'I will be older, in time. But with youth comes…' He took a few quick steps and a turn to indicate agility.

The Duke responded with a resigned sigh. Then he reached into the drawer of his desk and removed a stack of pound notes, counting out ten of them and setting them in a pile on the desk in front of him. 'I suppose, if I am to allow this fiasco at all, I want the best that money can buy.'

David nodded again, then eyed the money on the desk in a way that he hoped displayed a convincing amount of avarice.

'My sisters are very precious to me and I do not permit just anyone into their company.' He cleared his throat to draw David's attention away from the money. 'As you probably realise, men in your profession have a reputation for turning the heads of young girls.'

David shook his head violently. 'Your Grace, I would never—'

The Duke held up a hand.

'These girls are likely to be as much trouble as any man could be. I have sheltered them from society and they chafe under the restrictions.'

'I see,' David said, mentally cataloguing the weakness to exploit later.

'Your problem is just as likely to be other men, trying to reach them for clandestine meetings,' the Duke said, giving him a dead-eyed look. 'If there are suitors visiting during the day that I am unaware of, I would appreciate your telling me of them.'

'You want me to spy for you,' David said, nodding.

The Duke extended a fingertip and the pile of bills moved an inch further away. 'Nothing as vulgar as that. I simply want you to observe and report anything unusual that you might see.'

David could not see any difference between what he had said and the Duke's version, but now was not the time to argue. 'I will do as you ask,' he said with another nod and watched the money slide back to his side of the desk.

The Duke gave an encouraging nod and David picked up the notes and pocketed them.

'Of course, this brings us back to the matter we discussed at first,' the Duke said, 'and the dangers of having you in the house.'

'There will be no danger,' David assured him with a worried look.

'Good,' the Duke said, nodding back. 'See there is not. Because if I find that you have touched either of my sisters outside of what is necessary to teach them to waltz, I will kill you.'

The statement was delivered in such a casual way that, at first, David was not sure that he'd heard the words correctly. He started and stared back at the Duke, waiting to see if the man laughed, or winked, or gave any indication that he had been exaggerating.

Instead, the other man locked on to him with an unrelenting gaze, daring him to look away first.

For a moment, David forgot himself and stared back into the eyes of the murderer of his best friend, unwilling to yield. Then he remembered that the whole point of this charade was to gather information to prove his suspicions and reveal the truth to the world. That could not be done if he did not behave as a dancing master should. He dropped his eyes and offered a shallow bow. 'You have nothing to fear from me, *signor—scusi.* Your Grace. You have nothing to fear from me, Your Grace.' He bowed more deeply, as if humbled at the mistake in his address.

When he looked up, a slow smile spread across the Duke's face, stopping before it reached his eyes. 'That is good to know, Castellano. If I have no trouble from you, you will have no trouble from me. *Capisci?'*

'*Si,'* he said hurriedly, dipping his head again.

'My sisters are waiting for you in the music room.

Do not disappoint them. Or me.' He gave a vague gesture and pointed towards the door to indicate that the interview was over.

David backed away, allowing himself to bumble and stumble his way to the hall, but never taking his eyes from his adversary.

Once out of sight, he deliberately turned in the opposite direction of the way that had been indicated, trying to gain a quick tour of the ground floor. But a servant appeared almost immediately and directed him to the music room.

The two young ladies were waiting for him there. The elder, he had been informed, was Lady Olivia, a stately blonde with a cool beauty that could intimidate a man almost as quickly as her brother's threats. Her looks were paired with a quick mind, for she looked at him with the same direct stare her brother had given him, as if cataloguing strengths and weaknesses to exploit later.

As he had done to her brother, he smiled back and bowed deeply, doing everything in his power to appear harmless.

Then he turned to the younger of the two, Lady Margaret, and his false smile faltered.

She was looking back at him from sherry-brown eyes in a heart-shaped face framed in hair the colour of wild honey. Her exceptionally kissable mouth curved into a smile that made his heart stutter and his carefully laid plan shatter into a million pieces.

If he had tried to imagine the perfect woman, he

could not have done better than the one standing before him. Of course, his imagined paragon would not have been an unattainable goddess, miles above him in rank and the sister of his sworn enemy. In his fantasy, he'd have allowed himself some reason to hope instead of awakening the soul-gnawing envy he felt when facing down the upper classes.

He must hope that this woman would ruin his daydreams the moment she opened her mouth. If she was as shallow and silly as most of her set, he could ignore her physical appearance and forget his fantasies.

The disappointment of it would add steel to his resolve. He would strip every last bit of information he could from her unused brain without guilt or regret and use it to destroy her brother. Then she would see how the world treated those who had no powerful family to protect them from cruel reality.

Chapter Three

Peg should never have tried to outsmart her brother.

The promised dance master was standing before them now and, though he was not quite as disappointing as she feared he would be, he still seemed exceptionally foolish. Spending several hours a week with him would be almost as tedious as being alone.

At first glance, she would not have called Mr Castellano handsome. His hair oil was as thick as his accent, which was as false as his smile. His clothing was too tight, accentuating his long legs and thin waist, and making her look at places that no lady should be paying attention to. Everything about him was just a little too much to be taken seriously.

Most annoying, she had the fleeting impression that there was a perfectly ordinary man hiding underneath the fop. Or perhaps *ordinary* was not the word she was seeking, but *extraordinary*. His eyes were large and dark and his features strong and even. His shoulders were broad, his movements sure. And though his smile seemed overly bright to the point of mania, when he was not showing all of his brilliantly white teeth his mouth was very nice indeed.

It was as if he had downplayed his best qualities to make himself as unlikeable as possible.

Hugh had probably put him in mind to do that. She could not imagine him allowing a conventionally attractive man to have access to his sisters. She had been expecting him to find some man too decrepit to walk without a stick, much less dance. She imagined he would be ugly as well with straw-like grey hair and perhaps an embarrassingly large wart on his nose.

If Mr Castellano was truly handsome, he might be used to fathers and older brothers considering him a threat to a girl's virtue. For self-protection, he had made an effort to make himself ridiculous.

'*Buon giorno*, ladies,' the object of her curiosity said with a toothy grin. 'Today, we are learning to dance, no?'

'No,' her sister Olivia said, checking the little watch that was pinned to her gown. Then she reached into a pocket and removed a sovereign, tossing it to the dancing master who caught it instinctively. 'Hugh has left for Parliament by now and I will be going, as well.' She looked to the dancing master. 'There are more coins to come if you say nothing of this to anyone.'

'*Si, signora,*' he said, his head bobbing like a marionette with an unskilled puppeteer.

Then Liv walked to the window and opened it, throwing a leg over the sill and dropping from sight.

The dancing master stared after her, amazed.

'She has an assignation with her fiancé,' Peg supplied. 'Since our brother has not accepted the man's suit, it is not yet official. They are forced to meet in secret.'

When the man did not respond, she added, 'That is why she has bribed you not to tell him.'

Perhaps he did not understand her. He continued to stare at the open window, as if he expected her sister to reappear. *'So soltanto un po' di italiano. Lei parla inglese?'*

By the horrified and uncomprehending look he gave her in response to this, it was clear that he understood even less Italian than she did. She tried in English, so slowly that even a fool could understand. 'Olivia. Has gone.' She made a scurrying motion with her fingertips. 'Away.'

'I can see that,' he said, his accent faltering before he remembered where he was. 'Why did she not use the door?'

'Because our brother has men who watch the front and follow us when we go out,' Peg replied.

'How strange,' he said, still staring at the window.

'Not as strange as an Italian dancing master who cannot speak Italian.' She stared at him, her hands on her hips. 'It was clear that you could not answer me when I spoke to you. Why are you pretending to be someone who you are not?'

He blinked at her, as though it was necessary

to choose an appropriate answer to what seemed a simple question. Then he held his hands in the air, surrendering. 'It is because Ricardo Castellano can command a higher price as a dancing master than David Castell.'

She nodded in approval. She could not fault his logic. 'Does my brother know you are not Italian?'

'I suspect he does,' he said with a sad tilt of his head. 'My accent is not very good. But he did not bother to test my skill with the language to be sure.'

'Interesting,' she replied. 'He is normally so careful when it comes to us. I am surprised that he let a flaw in your character go unchallenged.'

The dancing master gave her a weak smile. 'I do not waste my time trying to understand the logic of the gentry.'

'I would think that understanding your employers was an important part of your job,' she said, staring back at him, intrigued.

He shrugged. 'It would be easier if they acted in a predictable manner. Unfortunately, they do not. I cannot explain your brother to you. Perhaps you could explain him to me.' He glanced at the open window again. 'For example, why did he bribe me far more than your sister did to report back to him the sort of thing that just happened?'

'He did what?'

'He gave me money to inform him if either of you sneaked out of the house to meet with men.'

Peg frowned. They had underestimated Hugh again. He had only given in to her request so he could add another layer of security to the hold he had on them. 'Well, that makes things clearer to me, at least,' she said and gave Mr Castell a resigned smile. 'How much did he offer you?' she asked.

'Ten pounds on top of my salary,' Mr Castell replied, blinking expectantly.

'And I suppose you will want more from us to keep Liv's activities secret.' Silently, Peg counted up the money she had saved from her allowance. It was not quite enough to equal what her brother had given him. Nor was she sure she wanted to waste every last penny of her own savings on furthering her sister's relationship with Mr Clement. If, after all the time he had been courting her, the man had not managed to persuade her sister into an elopement, Olivia could not be too firmly attached to him.

'We do not have to discuss that just yet,' he said. 'I do not know you well enough to decide which side of the battle I should take.'

The speculative look he was giving her made her flush pink before she remembered that it had never been her intention to fall for the flirtatious banter of a dancing master. If she wished to gain anything from the situation she had arranged, it would not do to have this stranger trying to manipulate her with sly smiles and warm glances.

Unless she could manage to do it to him first. She had little experience with flirting, but now might be an excellent time to practise it. She smiled back at him. 'Once you know Liv and I better, I am sure you will be sympathetic to our cause.' She allowed her lip to tremble, ever so slightly. 'Our brother is terribly strict with us, you see. And there is no reason for it, as we cause him no trouble and create no scandals.'

Mr Castell glanced at the window again, as if doubting that the missing Olivia could confirm her story.

'Though it may seem so, Olivia is not a flighty girl or careless with her reputation,' she said, tugging his sleeve to regain his attention. 'She has an understanding with the gentleman she is seeing today. He has offered for her multiple times and each time our brother has refused him.'

'There is probably a good reason for it,' Mr Castell said, sounding far too willing to give her brother the benefit of the doubt.

'None that we can find,' Peg insisted. 'Alister comes from a good family and has enough money to support them both. He has proven time and again that his affections are constant. If he has a flaw at all, it is that he is too meek and has been willing to wait for a change in my brother's heart rather than eloping to Scotland with Liv, ages ago.'

'And do you have suitors, as well?' he asked, then hurriedly added, 'Not that it is my business, of course. But it would be nice to have warning if you are planning to jump out a window as your sister did.'

'Certainly not,' she said with a laugh. 'Since I have not been allowed a Season, I have yet to meet a fellow who would want to lure me out of the house.'

'But you must be old enough,' he said.

'Nearly twenty,' she agreed. 'At first, it made

sense to postpone my come out, because we were in mourning for Father. But that cannot be the reason anymore.' She clamped her lips shut before she could reveal any more of her problems. She had never expected to be so free with a stranger, but Mr Castell was a surprisingly good listener.

'Do you suppose he means to spare you from gossip?' he said, eyes widening slightly.

'Gossip of what sort?' she said, shaking her head in denial and praying that he was not about to repeat the tired rumours about Hugh.

'When I took this job,' Mr Castell said carefully, 'friends reminded me that the Duke, your brother, is not well liked in many circles. People think him...' He paused again, as if hoping she would fill in the end of the sentence.

'You are speaking of the theory that he murdered our father,' she said, frowning to put him back in his place. 'Surely people are not still going on about that.' The foolishness of others had been part of the reason they had observed mourning so strenuously.

'It is not the sort of story that goes away,' Mr Castell said gently. 'In fact, it may have grown with time.'

It was not as if she had never heard the stories or seen the dark looks and whispers pass between the mothers of other girls in her limited acquaintance. But she had long ago learned to ignore them. 'People must find something more interesting to talk about,' she said, raising her chin. 'If they cannot, then perhaps Hugh is right to want to shield us. It must be very embarrassing for him to have the *ton* still spouting such nonsense.'

'They do not call him embarrassed,' Mr Castell supplied. 'I think the word most often used is *arrogant.*'

Peg winced. The description suited him. 'He does not suffer fools,' she said, secretly wishing that her brother was capable of being a little more agreeable.

'Nor does he make any effort to appear innocent,' the dancing master replied.

'He should not have to refute such a ridiculous accusation,' she snapped.

Mr Castell held his hands out in front of him, in a mollifying gesture. 'I am sorry to be the bearer of bad news. But I can only tell you what I have observed for myself.'

She could not help laughing at this. 'Observed? I am sorry, Mr Castell, but you are little more than a servant and newly hired at that. What could you possibly see that others closer to him did not?'

For a moment, the man's eyes narrowed as if he took her mention of his lack of status as an insult and not simply a statement of fact. It embarrassed her. She must have sounded terribly proud. Since he was the first man of any kind who had taken the time to speak to her, it was hardly fair of her to treat him badly.

His expression calmed again. When he spoke, it was in the same kind tone he had been using. 'After he offered me money to spy on your sister, he reminded me of my place, just as you did, just now.'

'I did not mean it,' she said hurriedly. 'It is just that you could not have met him before today, so how well could you possibly know him?'

'No offence was taken,' he said. But the bow that followed was stiff, as if he was unaccustomed to being quite as subservient as the situation required. Then he looked into her eyes again. 'I was surprised at his request to report on your activities, for it seemed a high-handed way to treat members of his family whom he claimed to care for.' He glanced at the window again. 'And I will admit, I admire you sister's method of thwarting him.'

'Most men who have met Olivia admire her for something or other,' Peg said, feeling ever so slightly jealous.

'She is beautiful, as well,' he agreed, still staring thoughtfully at the window. Then he turned suddenly back to her. 'As are you, of course.'

'Of course,' she said with a sigh.

'But I would never think to be forward with either of you,' he said hurriedly. 'It is a very foolish thing for a man in my position to become overly attached to his students. The situation would be improper. And quite hopeless.' He said the last words directly to her and with an answering sigh of regret that made her feel instantly better about being everyone's second choice of sisters.

'Since I understand my place,' he said, bowing again, 'he had no reason to threaten to kill me, as he did.'

'He did what?' she said with surprise.

'He informed me that if I touched either of his sisters, he would kill me,' Mr Castell replied.

'He was only trying to frighten you,' she said, raising a hand to her mouth to hide the smile that was spreading there.

But Mr Castell did not seem the least bit cowed by the threat. His eyes were narrowed again and his chin squared, as if ready to meet a challenge. It made him look far more formidable than the man she had dismissed as silly only a short time before. 'He was sincere in his threat,' Castell said. 'I have spoken with such men before and can tell the difference between a playful exaggeration and a man who might be capable of violence.'

Peg shook her head. She understood that people were suspicious of him over Father's death. But the idea that they might really believe her brother when he spoke thus had never occurred to her. 'He should learn to moderate his speech. He has said things similar before and will likely say them again. I believe he even threatened Alister in that way, when he sent him off after the failed proposal.' She glanced into the garden, wishing that Olivia was there for reassurance, then shrugged. 'I know you are unlikely to meet him, but I can assure you that it has been some time and Alister Clement is alive and healthy as ever he was.'

'Because your brother does not know he is still around,' Castell finished for her.

'Now that you know, do you mean to tell him?'

she asked, surprised to feel a finger of dread trace down her spine.

'What can you give me to keep the secret?' he asked, giving her a long, slow look as he waited for the answer.

'I do not have very much money,' she said, feeling strangely vulnerable under his gaze.

He took a step towards her, moving with the grace of the dancer she had expected. 'There is something you have which is more valuable than gold.'

Her eyes widened. Though he had assured her he would take no liberties, he seemed to be speaking of something so wicked that she could hardly believe he had said it aloud, much less done it on the first day they'd met. Perhaps these dancing lessons would be much more exciting than she had anticipated.

Now that his disguise had been penetrated, it was much easier to see the handsome man beneath the foppish exterior. She stared into his dark eyes, trying to imagine what it might be like to be kissed by him.

Then, he answered the question she was afraid to ask in a way that was far more mundane than she'd imagined. 'You could give me your trust.'

'What?' she said, confused.

'I understand that you love your brother and do not want to think ill of him,' he said. 'But from what I have seen today, I cannot help worrying about the safety of you and your sister.'

'That is kind of you,' she said, trying not to sound disappointed. 'But your concern is not necessary. We are both fine.'

'Perhaps now you are,' he said. 'But if things change, or if you feel afraid for any reason, you must tell me. I will do everything in my power to help you.'

It was an unusual request and agreeing to it cost her nothing. But she did not see what he would have to gain in helping someone he had just met. Perhaps he was just a good person who cared deeply about others. If there was another, more devious reason, she could not think what it might be.

'I doubt there will be anything to tell you,' she said. 'But I will agree, as long as you promise not to tell Hugh about Olivia and Alister. I do not know what he will do if he realises that we have tricked him.' She regretted the words immediately for they came out sounding far too dire and seemed to contradict everything she had just said.

If Mr Castell had noticed the fact, he did her the courtesy of pretending he had not. 'It will be our secret,' he agreed, giving her another smile that was nothing like the insincere grins he had begun with. The idea that they had a shared secret gave an intimacy to it, making her feel that he had known her for ages and not just a few minutes.

Hesitantly, she smiled back at him and felt a jolt of connection that had not been there before. Without thinking, she took a step closer to him, until they were almost near enough to dance, as she had assumed they would when he had first come to her.

Suddenly, there was a whistle from the window. The distraction broke the bond between them and Peg ran to help boost her sister back into the room.

Olivia was flushed and happy, as if she had spent her time dancing about the room, just as had been expected of her.

She looked between Peg and the dancing master and her smile became a suspicious frown.

'It is all right,' Peg whispered back to her. 'We have an understanding.'

'I believe it is time for me to be going.' Now that Liv had returned, the false Italian accent, the broad smile and mocking subservience had returned, as well. But when he turned to bow to Peg, he winked as he did it, to remind her that only she knew the truth about him.

It was only when he had left them alone in the music room that Peg realised they had not danced at all.

Chapter Four

In some ways, the investigation was going better than he had hoped. On their first meeting, the Duke had incriminated himself from his own lips with the threat of murder. His sister had confirmed that he had a habit of making such promises and hinted at the dissatisfaction of both girls with the way their brother isolated them. And the older girl had given him blackmail material without even bothering to speak to him. If information continued to flow so freely from the family, he would have answers in no time at all.

But if he had hoped that Margaret Bethune would disappoint him and make the morality of his job easier, this was not to be the case. He left the town house feeling unsettled, almost to the point of guilt. It had not bothered him to lie to Scofield—for that man deserved whatever he got—but the girls had done nothing to him. Neither had they done anything for him. He had known them for less than an hour. It pained him more than it should have to deceive them. One of them, at least.

Lady Olivia had been just as he had expected her to be, aloof and ready to dismiss him as unimportant without bothering to take a second glance. Of course, he could not really blame her for trying to get away from the Duke. It proved that she was aware of the danger she was in and looking for a way out. He would not prevent her from escaping and would help her if he could. If, in the future, he needed to exploit her vulnerability, he would do so with little hesitation.

But Lady Margaret was another matter. He had hoped that she would disappoint him and reveal a dull mind and a bland personality. Instead, she had seen through his disguise almost immediately and forgiven him for the deception. Still, she had chatted amiably with him, not afraid to share details of her life. She had spoken to him almost as if he was her equal.

It was only when he had threatened her brother that she had shown him the side of her character that he had expected to see. She had been quick to remind him that he was a nobody and, surprisingly, it had stung. He had come very close to announcing that he was far more than a mere dancing master. Then he had remembered that his true identity would not have impressed her, either.

It was a shame. She was everything he admired in a woman and more than just a beauty. Perhaps it was because her brother had sheltered her from the *ton.* There was a freshness about her, like coming upon a newly opened rose. Her eyes were wide and guileless, but there was intelligence in them, as well.

He might have done a better job of maintaining his *nom de guerre* had he not been slack-jawed by her beauty as she'd questioned him in Italian. Lord knew how he would manage when he actually had to dance with her. As it was, he had taken far too much pleasure in talking with her and he'd felt a surprising disappointment when her sister had reappeared and put an end to it.

It concerned him that she seemed to have no idea that her brother was truly dangerous. She had an excuse for everything, putting all she had seen and heard off as loose talk and coincidence. Though she had no complaints about Scofield, other than that he was strict, David could not help worrying about her, trapped in a house with a villain.

He wanted to rescue her.

He shook his head. When had he become prone to daydreaming of himself as some sort of hero? He must put such musings out of his mind and remember that, no matter what else was true, she was the sister of a duke. Such girls might smile at their dancing masters, but they would never entertain the advances of the bastard son of a minor lord, who made his living writing for a newspaper.

That thought depressed him more than it should have. He would do well to remember that any friendship they might have was only temporary. She would actively hate him when he revealed to all of London that her brother was a murderer.

And when he did so, what would happen to her? Society could be cruel enough to girls whose families broke even the smallest rules. The world would be merciless if their brother was stripped of his title and hanged. No men of rank would have the girls to wife. The other best option, ladylike employment as a governess or tutor, would be impossible, as well. Families would think twice before hiring someone with such a notorious bloodline.

He shook his head again, rejecting the doubts that were growing there. It should not matter to him what happened, since he had known Lady Margaret Bethune for less than an hour. But that did not mean he wanted to bring about the downfall of an innocent girl. Perhaps, if he helped Lady Olivia towards an elopement before the article was published, she would take her younger sister into her new home and see to it that she had a future.

For the next lesson, he waited until he was sure that Scofield had left the house before making his appearance. Then, after assuring the footman at the door that he knew where he was going, he purposely turned wrong, finding his way back to the study, where the old Duke's body had been found. He had worried that he might find the room locked, but the door was open and a maid was rubbing down the woodwork with beeswax and lemon.

'*Scusi,*' he said, giving her a bow and a smile. 'I am lost, I think.'

The maid smiled back, giggling. 'You are the new dancing master for the ladies? I will be done here in a moment and will take you to the music room myself.' She shuddered. 'I welcome the company. I do not like being in this room alone.'

'Why not?' he said, giving her another smile and a wide-eyed look.

'The place is haunted,' she said, her eyes just as wide.

'No.' He shook his head in mock amazement. 'By whom?'

'The last Duke died in that very spot,' she said, pointing a finger at the seat behind the desk.

'And now his son sits in his chair,' David said to her. 'Is he not bothered by it?'

'You would think so, but he does not turn a hair,' she said, just as amazed.

'And how did the old Duke die?' he said, asking the question that needed no answer.

'Murder,' the maid replied, with obvious relish. 'A letter opener to the heart.' She mimed the strike and collapse.

He shuddered in appreciation. 'Did they catch the killer?'

At this, her eyes went even wider and she seemed to realise that she had spoken too freely in front of a stranger. She went to the door and looked out to make sure that there was no one in the hall that might overhear. She came back to him and whispered, 'We all know who it was that done it. And that is all I'm saying. Those on the staff that had a place to go to either gave notice or just run off, rather than work for the young Duke. If I could find a new position, I'd be gone, too.'

'Really?' he said, a little surprised at how quickly the staff turned against him when the Duke was gone. 'And do you have any proof?' He held his breath, wondering if it could truly be this easy.

'Who else could it have been?' the maid said. 'That night, the study window was open, but it leads to a fenced garden. No one was seen coming or going. And Lady Olivia's dog, which will not shut up under the best of circumstances, did not let out a single bark to warn of an intruder.'

'How strange,' he agreed, disappointed that the evidence was not more concrete.

'It was someone in the house what done it,' the maid announced with a confident nod. 'The new Duke did nothing but argue with his father for the whole of their lives together. Who else could it have been?'

'That is damning,' he agreed. 'But did anyone see anything?'

'See anything?' Her eyes went wide. 'I scrubbed the blood from the rug myself. That was more than anyone would want to see.'

'Of course,' he said, doing his best to hide his frustration. It seemed that inside the house, just as out of it, everyone was sure they knew the truth, but no one had solid evidence to prove it.

The sharp sound of a cleared throat came from the doorway. When David looked towards it, he saw Lady Margaret, arms folded and looking stern. 'Did you lose your way, Mr Castellano?'

David shrugged and gave her a broad grin. 'The young lady said she would help me to the door when she had time.'

'She need not trouble herself,' the girl said with a glint in her eye that looked almost like jealousy. 'I will show you to the music room myself.' This last was delivered more as a command than an offer of assistance.

'Of course,' David said, then added, *'Grazie'*, and another ingratiating smile in the direction of the maid.

When they were clear of the study door, Lady Margaret looked back at him, frowning. 'Do not claim that you were lost to me, Mr Castell. It is not that hard to find the music room.'

He shrugged and gave her an embarrassed smile. 'Perhaps I turned wrong on purpose.'

'Because you are curious about my brother,' she reminded him.

'I met him in that room on the last visit,' he admitted. 'I thought perhaps he would expect me to report on our progress.'

'Then I cannot imagine why you were there, since we have made none,' she reminded him. 'You were not going to report on Olivia, were you?'

'I promised I would not,' he said, putting his hand on his heart to show the depths of his loyalty. They had reached the music room and she ushered him in and shut the door behind them, leaving them alone. 'I assume your sister has already left us?' he said, glancing towards the window.

'She had an appointment and could not wait for you to appear,' Lady Margaret said, chiding him for his late arrival. 'Perhaps, if you had not spent so much time flirting with the maid...'

'That was not what I was doing,' he replied, before realising that it would have been a much better explanation than the truth.

'It does not signify,' she said, obviously still annoyed, but holding up her hands to stop further justifications. 'But I am sure, if my brother is paying you for these lessons, he would prefer you to spend some of your time with me.'

'Of course, Lady Margaret,' he replied, trying not to grin. She was actually jealous of the time he had spent talking to a servant. The reporter in him should be pleased that she had been distracted from asking questions about their conversation. But the man in him was too busy being flattered that she would even care.

Now she was staring at him expectantly, obviously waiting for him to say something more. Perhaps it was her beauty that was confounding him, but he had no idea how to proceed.

'I thought, perhaps, this time we might try some dancing,' she said, a smile flickering on her lips as if pleased with his befuddlement.

'Of course,' he said. Dancing. It was what he had

come here to teach, after all. It suddenly occurred to him that his experience was likely more limited than hers. When he did have the opportunity to stand up with a lady, he never paid attention to what they did on their side of the line. Was it different, or merely the reverse of their partner's moves?

'You have more experience than I with how these lessons are to go,' she said, with the intense gaze of a rapt pupil. 'Will you be providing the music?'

'Music?' he said, annoyed at the stupidity of the repetition.

'To dance to,' she reminded him. 'The pianoforte is in good tune.'

'I do not play,' he said, embarrassed. Then added, 'Do you?'

'Of course,' she replied. 'But I cannot play and dance at the same time.'

'Of course not,' he said, shaking his head. Why had he not considered the details of this disguise before entering into it? 'Counting,' he blurted, relieved. 'The music is not needed if we can count to eight. I will do the counting and you will do the steps.'

She smiled and nodded in agreement. 'Of course. I should have thought of that.' She took a step away from him and turned back with a graceful sweep of her skirts and a curtsy as if readying herself to join a set. 'And what dance will you be teaching me today?'

What dances did he know? 'Sir Roger de Coverly,' he muttered, trying to remember the order of the steps.

Her face fell. 'As a review, perhaps. But I know it quite well and do not really need instruction.'

'Hole in the Wall,' he corrected.

'That is also familiar to me,' she said. 'I can show you, if you want.'

It would buy him some time, as he thought of a different dance. 'Very good,' he said. 'Demonstrate. And one, and two, and three…'

She closed her eyes as if imagining a room full of people and moved flawlessly through the steps of the dance, humming the tune softly to herself to keep the beat. And, as he had on their last meeting, he felt his distraction growing and his true goals fading further away. His hand raised, palm out to touch hers as it passed, leading her in a circle before returning to home and bowing to her as she finished.

Her eyes popped open, surprised at his touch, smiling eagerly as she looked for his approval.

As he nodded, he could not help grinning back at her. 'Lovely. Your dancing, that is,' he added, struggling for a coherent thought.

'Thank you.' She bobbed another curtsy, and blushed back at him, pleased with his compliment.

'Show me more,' he said. The sly part of him cheered at the time-wasting distraction, but another growing part of his heart just wanted to see her dance again.

She danced through the changes of a cotillion, then switched gracefully to the steps of a Scottish reel. And as she moved before him, he forgot that his reason in coming was to question her about the murders. The very idea of that seemed so sordid that it embarrassed him to consider it. For now, he wanted to let his mind float free as he admired a pretty girl.

By the time she was finished with her demonstration, most of the hour had passed. She ended with a final twirl to stand directly in front of him, eyes still closed, as if she did not want to leave the imagined ball that she was attending.

He could see himself there, with her, dancing until they were exhausted, then searching out a quiet corner to sit together for a moment of stolen intimacy, shaded from the rest of the party by a potted palm. The dream was so sweet that he forgot she was not sharing it and leaned forward, kissing her on the tip of the nose.

Her eyes flew open and she started back, surprised. 'I did not give you permission to do that.'

'I do not know what came over me,' he said honestly. But though she might be about to ban him from the house, he could not seem to regret what he had done. Then, he added, 'Did you mind it so very much?'

'I do not know,' she said, colouring so sweetly that he wanted to kiss her again. 'I have never been kissed by a man before and I do not know how I am supposed to react.'

'There is no one correct way to respond,' he said. 'If I upset you, do not be afraid to tell me. But if you were hoping for a more profound experience, that was hardly a kiss at all. I do not think you need count it as your first.'

'Oh,' she said, her voice a strange mix of relief and disappointment. Then she tipped her head to the side, considering. 'And just what do you think an appropriate first kiss should be like?'

It was a dangerous question, but it was an invitation that he could not resist taking. He thought for a moment, then looked into her eyes and tried to imagine what it might be like to kiss her again. 'I do not know if I have ever given one before. But I would think a great deal of care must be taken, to make it worthy of the lady's expectations. It needs to be memorable.'

She let out a little sigh, as she savoured the fantasy of the kiss he described. 'Do go on.'

'It must be both gentle, in respect of her inexperience, but passionate enough to give her a hint of what is to come, should she want a second kiss.'

'It sounds as though you have an excellent grasp of the particulars,' she said, swallowing nervously, but making no effort to move away from him.

'Would you like a practical demonstration?' he asked, praying for the answer he wanted to hear.

'Well, it is not as if you are teaching me to dance,' she said, her eyes sparkling. 'I must learn something so that you are worthy of what my brother pays you.'

'True,' he said, throwing caution aside and placing his hands on her shoulders and drawing her closer to him.

Suddenly, there was a whistle from the window, announcing the return of Lady Olivia.

David snatched his hands away and took a quick step back, turning away to compose himself before the other girl appeared.

Margaret did something similar, pressing her hands to her hot cheeks, then running them quickly down her skirts to smooth away evidence of a passionate interlude that had only occurred in their imaginations. Then she went to the window and hauled her sister back into the house.

Olivia looked much as she had after the last lesson, as if she had spent an hour in the arms of her lover. And as she had then, she looked back and forth between the two of them, as if it were possible for her to discern what had occurred with a single glance. But this time, she raised an eyebrow, as if she had found something that interested her.

She clasped her hands together in a gesture of finality. 'Well, then. Another excellent lesson, Mr Castellano.'

'Thank you,' he said, not bothering with an accent.

She gave a single blink of surprise at the change in his voice, then added, 'Can you see yourself out, or shall I have a footman show you the door?'

'I will take him,' Margaret said hurriedly. 'He has been known to get lost in the house.'

'That will not be necessary,' he assured them both, backing towards the door. 'I can find my own way.' To this he added a deep bow, so that only Margaret could see the grin on his face. 'Until the next time, my lady?'

'Of course,' she said with a smile, holding the door for him and closing it after he was through.

Once Mr Castell was gone and they were alone together, Liv turned to Peg with a knowing grin. 'And how was today's dancing lesson?'

'Fine,' Peg said hurriedly, wondering how much of their activities she should admit to. 'He is not Italian, of course.'

'Very few of them are,' Liv said with a knowing nod.

'His real name is David Castell.' Then she added, 'Hugh bribed him to spy on you and report if you escaped from the house to see Alister.'

This announcement wiped the smug smile from her sister's face. 'He told you this?'

'You do not have to worry,' Peg said, with a superior smile. 'We discussed it. He pities us for the restrictions that have been placed on us and is more concerned for our safety than he is in obeying Hugh.'

'You discussed it,' her sister said, regaining some of her control. 'Did you do this while you were dancing?'

'Actually—' Peg said, then stopped, searching for a way to explain.

'You have been too busy talking to do much dancing,' Liv finished for her.

Peg could feel her cheeks going pink as she answered with an embarrassed nod.

As if sensing the reason for her blush, Liv laughed. 'Has something already happened that you do not want to admit to?'

'He kissed me,' she admitted, then added, 'On the nose.'

'That is hardly a kiss at all,' Liv said, agreeing with Mr Castell. 'Better luck next time.'

'You should not say such things,' Peg scolded back. 'You should probably tell Hugh and have him banned from the house.' She held her breath, praying that her sister would do no such thing.

'Since he is keeping my secret, it would be very foolish of me to report such a minor lapse in judgement,' Liv said with a shrug. 'Besides, it is rather tiresome to be the only sister getting into mischief in this family.'

'It cannot really be making trouble if you are only seeing Alister,' Peg said.

'I am sure Hugh would think otherwise,' Liv said with a giggle. 'I had a very nice hour with Alister. He kissed me twice.'

For a moment, Peg remembered what Mr Castell had said about Hugh's ignorance of Alister figuring in his continued good health. Hopefully, he and her sister would find a way to marry before they were discovered. 'You have known him for quite some time,' Peg said. 'I am not surprised that he kisses you. But is he any closer to taking you away to Scotland?'

Liv responded with a defiant look. 'An elopement is hardly a suitable wedding for the sister of a duke. We are waiting to be married properly, in a church. I am sure Hugh will relent eventually. It is just a matter of time.'

'That is a futile hope and you know it,' Peg replied. 'Our brother is not known for his changeable nature.'

'But it is my hope, all the same,' Liv said with a sigh. 'You would understand if you had ever had the opportunity to meet anyone who puts your heart at risk.'

'That is probably true,' Peg replied, surprised at how quickly an image of Mr Castell appeared in her mind. But what did that have to do with wanting a church wedding, rather than an elopement? Surely, if one was truly in love, they would be too far lost in it to care where, or when, or even if they married.

'Now you are truly blushing,' her sister said with another laugh. She held up a hand to stop Peg's objections before they could begin. 'If you are considering a flirtation with the dancing master, I would not begrudge it to you.'

'He is rather handsome,' Peg agreed, at last. Although she wished he would not use quite so much hair oil. She had an illogical desire to run her hands through it and loosen the curls.

Liv nodded in approval. 'With his tight pants and his fake accent, I am sure he is aware of the effect he has on young girls. It is how he makes his living, after all. As long as you do not take him too seriously, you will have a lovely time letting him flirt with you.'

Was that what she was to him? Just another in a long line of pretty faces? Then why had he seemed both surprised and delighted by the simple peck on the nose he had given her today? 'That is very calculated of you,' Peg replied at last.

'Of course it is, little sister. But, since Hugh will not allow you a Season, it is up to me to tell you the truths you might have learned from the *ton*. While people claim that they want young women to seem guileless, it is never in our best interests to actually be so. There are very few liberties allowed to an unmarried girl, but if one is careful, rules can be bent quite a distance before they are broken.'

She wanted to argue that she had no intention of being so foolish, right under her brother's nose. But then she remembered the kiss she most certainly would have got if her sister had been just a few moments later. 'Suppose what you say is true,' Peg said. 'What would be the best way to go about bending the rules?'

'Make sure that your Mr Castell teaches you to waltz,' Liv said. 'And do not allow him to maintain a polite distance as he dances. Stumble as often as you need to so he must hold you tightly.'

It was exactly what her sister should be warning her against, but it was exactly what she wanted to do. 'I will keep that in mind if we dance together for my next lesson,' she said.

'If you dance?' Liv said, surprised.

'When we dance,' Peg corrected. 'It is not as if nothing has been accomplished, so far. Today, I demonstrated the dances that I already knew.'

Her sister stared back at her, obviously puzzled.

'It sounds as if you are the one teaching the lessons and not him.'

'Do not tell Hugh,' she said quickly.

'I would not think of it,' Liv promised.

'He is very nice,' she admitted. 'And if Hugh finds out that he is not doing his job, I would not want anything to happen to him.' Why had she expressed it in that way? It put her in mind of Mr Castell's comments about their brother's habit of threatening people with death. 'I don't want to see him dismissed before we've even had a chance to begin,' she corrected herself.

'Then you had best be sure you have learned something when Hugh comes sniffing around for a demonstration,' Liv said.

'And what of you? You have not even been here.'

'I know how to dance well enough to fool him,' her sister said with a shrug. 'You are the novice who asked for the lessons. See to it that, when Hugh asks to see what you have learned, you do not appear to have gained knowledge in anything but the Boulanger and the quadrille. Beyond that, what the Duke does not know will not hurt any of us.'

Chapter Five

The next morning at breakfast, Peg sat on her end of the table enjoying her morning chocolate, while her brother kept his place at the head, deeply engrossed in a newspaper and a coffee. As usual, her sister had slept in and taken tea and toast in her room, leaving the two of them alone.

For the most part, Peg enjoyed mornings with her brother. They rarely spoke, but neither did they argue. It was a time of peaceful communion between the two of them that reminded her of carefree days in the nursery, when they were children.

Of course, when they were younger, Hugh had not spent so much time with his nose buried in a newspaper, nor was he as easily annoyed by what he read. Now, the paper in his hand rattled and he made a series of angry huffing noises before slapping it down on the table. 'Damned muckrakers,' he said, shaking his head.

'Is the news bad?' Peg asked, trying not to smile at his overreaction.

'Nothing you need to worry about,' he said, folding the paper so that the offending article was hidden. 'It merely annoys me to see ignorant commentary on things I have said in Parliament, from a man who clearly knows nothing at all about government.'

'You should know better than to read such things during a meal,' she said, taking a piece of toast from the rack. 'They will only upset your digestion.'

'That is probably true,' he said, taking a sip of his coffee. 'Let us turn our minds to more pleasant topics. How are you enjoying your dancing lessons?'

Before she could stop it, she felt a blush creeping into her cheeks. Fortunately, her brother was as uninterested in making actual chit-chat as he usually was and did not look up from his breakfast to see it.

'Fine,' she said. 'I am enjoying the lessons and thank you for the privilege.'

'And is your sister enjoying them, as well?' Now he surprised her, meeting her gaze with a pointed look, as if ready to catch her in a lie.

'I think she is quite satisfied with them,' Peg answered truthfully. 'But you would have to ask her.'

'I suspect I shall,' he said, not looking away. 'But for now, I am speaking with you. I know your sister is headstrong and eager to escape the house. I would hope, if she is doing something she shouldn't, that you would tell me.'

If this was an attempt to coerce her into spying for him, it failed utterly. She chose her next words carefully, so as to answer honestly without betraying Liv. 'I think, if you were less strict with her, she would not want to rebel.'

He grunted in response and picked up the paper again. 'I do not remember asking your opinion.'

'Perhaps you should have,' she said, smiling back at him. 'Since I am one, I know far more about young women than you do. I can assure you you will never keep either of us in line by tightening the restrictions on us.'

She remembered what Mr Castell had said about the possible reasons that their brother kept them from the *ton*. 'If you are concerned that we might be as bothered by gossip as you are by your newspaper, you must not worry. I know better than to believe nonsense told to us by others, or to be hurt by cuts and snubs from ignorant strangers.'

He looked up at her, more shocked than surprised, searching her expression, as if wondering if they were thinking of the same scandal.

'I do not think you need to worry about such a thing, but all the same it is a very sensible response,' he said, raising his paper again to block her out and indicate that further speculation about his motives was not welcome.

But this only served to take him back to the thing that had made him angry before. As she finished her toast, he let out another series of huffs and gave the paper a vicious shake as if it might rearrange the words to be more to his liking. 'Damned Castell,' he muttered.

'I beg your pardon,' she said, sure that she could not have heard him correctly.

He huffed again. 'And I beg yours. I should not use such language in your presence.'

'Were you swearing at someone in particular?' she said, waiting for the correction that would prove she had misheard him.

'It is nothing,' he said, rattling the paper again.

'It did not sound like nothing.'

'Just a reporter who never fails to annoy me,' he said, setting the paper aside. 'It is foolish of me to keep reading his articles, since it is likely to drive me to apoplexy one day. That is probably what he is hoping for, since he never has a fair word to say about me.'

'I see,' she said, eyeing the paper.

Her brother took a deep sip from his coffee, then pushed the cup aside. 'But enough of that. I have far more important things to worry about than the opinions of a scribbler in a second-rate newspaper.' He rose from the table then and left her.

She waited only a moment for him to get clear of the door before grabbing the paper and paging through it to find the article that had angered him. It was a review of the recent doings in Parliament and highly critical of the position her brother had taken. And the name under the headline was just as she had feared: David Castell.

She dropped the paper on the table again. Perhaps it was a common name. There must be more than one Castell family in England and surely there could be more than one of them named David. Since her dancing master had not bothered to spell it for her, perhaps it was not the same name at all.

But in her heart, she knew it must be true. The coincidence of his arrival was just too great. It also explained how she had managed to get a dancing master who did not actually dance.

But that led to the question of just what it was he had come to find. The answer was obvious. He was the one that had brought up the rumours still swirling about her brother. He had also been quick to tell her that her brother had sent him to spy on them. Was that the truth, or merely something he had made up to win her loyalties?

Worst of all, he had kissed her. It was not much of a kiss, but it was probably the beginning of a plot to seduce her, using her fickle heart to make her betray her family.

The murder had been almost two years ago. When would scandalmongers like David Castell give up their speculations and realise that the real killer would never be found?

There was one way to find out. Without realising it, she had crumpled the paper in her hands. Now she smoothed it, folded it and tucked it under her arm. She must prepare for today's dance lesson. Perhaps Mr Castell would have to prepare himself for a few unfortunate truths, as well.

David arrived at the Scofield town house that day trying not to be too eager for the lesson that was to come. It was probably for the best that the last visit with Lady Margaret had been interrupted by her sister. He had been on the verge of abandoning his true mission in favour of a dalliance with someone who was young, innocent and totally out of reach.

Rationally, he knew nothing could come of it. He might steal a few kisses, but he would leave soon and never see her again. Still, there was a dangerous part of his heart that wanted more, just as he wanted a better hand than he'd been dealt in every other part of his life. Where was it written that some people were born deserving less than their fellows? Had God put a woman like Margaret Bethune on the planet simply to remind him that his aspirations were doomed to failure?

He forced himself to remember his true purpose, which was to make war and not love. Ruining Scofield would not just avenge Dick Sterling. The article might also be the making of David's career. His father could hardly ignore him if his investigative work made him the talk of London. Margaret Bethune had no part in any of that, other than as a source of information.

There was also the fact that Scofield would kill him if he found out about the simple kiss that David had already given her. Try as he might, he could not manage to be frightened by the fact. In truth, he felt it would be better to die for a larger sin than one as pathetically small as that had been.

His plan for the day was to limit himself to a few weak dance lessons, ferreting out more information about the family as he led her through the steps. If something of a romantic nature developed from that? He could not help the grin that was spreading across his face. A few kisses would do neither of them harm and would give Margaret a bit of the adventure she had been denied by her scoundrel of a brother.

Today he made no effort to lose himself in wrong turns, but arrived at the music room promptly on the hour in time to see Lady Olivia disappearing out the window with the help of her sister. When Lady Margaret turned back from the window, he greeted her with a broad smile and a deep bow. 'I have been counting the hours, my lady,' he said, embarrassed at the sincerity in his voice.

'Have you now?' she said, with none of her usual warmth. She reached into the pocket of her gown and produced a folded sheet of newsprint, waving it once in his face before slapping him in the chest with it and stalking towards the middle of the room.

He did not have to read it to realise that she must have found his latest editorial from the newspaper. 'I had no idea you read the *Standard*,' he said, trying a more tentative, playful smile.

'You must think me so stupid that I could not read at all,' she snapped. 'Of course, I am probably as great a fool as you think me, since I did not immediately report to my brother that you had a false name, a false accent and no dancing ability whatsoever.'

'I do not think you foolish in the least,' he assured her. 'And, all things considered, I thought we were getting along quite well together without my having to dance for you.'

'Because I did not know who you were,' she said, spitting out the words as though they were coated in vinegar. 'If I had known you were playing up to me so that I would tell you family secrets, I'd have told Hugh that you kissed me. Then you could find out for yourself if he is truly a dangerous man.'

It was a perfectly reasonable response to what he had done. But what surprised him most was the fact that she had not already carried it out. If she was truly angry at him, he'd have thought that her brother would already have a hand on his collar, leading him to his fate.

'You have nothing to say for yourself?' she said, outraged.

'I am sorry that I have lied to you,' he said, trying and failing to find the words to describe how he felt about deceiving her. 'But I am doing what I am doing for the good of society.'

'You think the world requires you to harass an innocent man and enter our home under false pretences to lure information out of me by lying?' she said. 'I had no idea that the greater good was so despicable.'

For a moment he looked into her eyes and felt the hurt of his betrayal as keenly as she did. Then, he remembered it was not just the murder of the Duke he sought to avenge, but his friend's, as well. 'It gave me no feeling of pride to mislead you,' he said, hardening his heart. 'You are innocent of all this. But though you want to believe it so, your brother is not. It is not only your father whom he killed. He murdered a close friend of mine, stabbed him and threw his body in the river like garbage.'

'Did you see it happen?'

'No,' he admitted. 'But I know that they argued and I know that Scofield threatened to kill him. Two days later, Dick was dead—murdered, just as your brother had promised.'

'Then you know as much as you claim to know about Father's death and that is nothing at all,' she snapped. 'All you have is rumour, assumption and my brother's tendency to threaten people. But since you do not know him, you cannot know the truth. He would never follow through on his words.'

'Yet people he threatens tend to die,' David reminded her.

'A coincidence,' she snapped. 'He had nothing to do with either of those deaths.'

'Murders,' David corrected, unable to let her hide from the truth.

'Murders, then,' she said, obviously frustrated with his clarification. 'But that still does not mean Hugh had anything to do with them.'

'We will have to disagree,' he said, for it was clear there was nothing he could say that would persuade her of the disaster about to strike her family. 'But that does not tell me what you mean to do, now that you have discovered my secret.'

At this question, her anger evaporated, replaced with confusion. It was clear that she had no plan, other than the initial confrontation with him. She stared at him in silence for a moment as she tried to calculate her next move. Then she said, 'If it makes you feel better, I will not tell him what you really came here to do.'

'Thank you,' he said, surprised. Considering how she must feel about him, it was more than he deserved.

'But neither will I allow you to libel my brother,' she added.

'It is not libel, if it is the truth,' David reminded her.

She released a frustrated sigh. 'What if I can prove to you that he is innocent?'

'Then I would most like to hear it.' He leaned closer. 'What do you know?' She had been in the house at the time of the crime. Perhaps there was something she remembered that would prove her support for Scofield was more than just family loyalty.

But now that she was pressed for details, she had fallen silent again. 'I will find something,' she said at last. 'Then you will see that you are wrong.'

'You would not know where to look,' he said.

'Neither would you,' she reminded him. 'Yet you came to this house, ready to search.'

'I assumed I would find someone to help me,' he said, wondering if she knew how little effort it had taken to get information out of her own servants.

'I suppose you wanted me to help you ruin my own brother,' she said, disgusted. 'You were trying to turn me against him on the first day we met.'

'My warnings on that day were sincere,' he said. 'I was and am worried for you and your sister, left in the care of a man who might be capable of anything. If you were afraid to be in the house with him, I wanted to know.'

'Well, I am not,' she said. 'I am more concerned with the wild lies you will be spreading if you do not have someone to see that you have the whole story.'

'Then help me,' he said. 'If you are right and I am wrong, find one piece of evidence that will support the fact and I will drop my plans and leave Scofield in peace.'

She stared at him, biting her lip, and said, 'All right. If an investigation is going to take place, I want to be involved in it. But only because I know he is innocent and I mean to prove it to you.'

'You will help?' he said, surprised that he had got her to agree.

'It is better that I do it willingly than that you trick me into it,' she said with a sigh. 'And it will be easier for all of us if I do not go to Hugh and insist that I no longer want the lessons I asked him for. He will ask questions that none of us wants to answer.'

She was speaking of his lies, Olivia's escapes and the kiss he had already given her. In a few short visits, they had created a complicated web of potential blackmail that no one wanted to unravel. 'I will keep your secrets if you keep mine,' he assured her. 'Together, perhaps we can uncover the truth.'

She nodded, resigned, then glanced at the clock

on the mantle. 'We have half a lesson left. Where do
you wish to begin?'

'You want to start now?' he said, surprised.

'We might as well get it over with,' she said with
another sigh. 'What can I help you with?'

'I would like to meet your sister's dog,' he said.

'No,' she replied, firmly. 'I do not think you would.'

'Why would you say that?' he said, smiling.

'Because no one wants to meet that horrid little beast. At least, no one wants to meet him twice.
Once is usually enough to form a permanent dislike of him.'

'That is precisely why I want to see him. Where
is this dog and why have I not seen him already?'

'Because, on occasions when my sister does not
want to deal with him, which is most of the time, he
is kept in a kennel in the back garden.'

'Show me,' he said again, moving to the window
that Olivia used to escape.

Lady Margaret reached out and tugged him back.
'Let us use a more conventional method of exit.'

'What will you tell the staff, if they enquire as to
what we are doing?'

'I will think of something,' she said with a shrug
and led him out of the room and down a corridor towards the kitchen. As they passed through to get to
the back door, the cook gave them a fish-eyed look.

'Mr Castellano says he is fond of dogs. I am taking
him to meet Caesar to disabuse him of that.'

The cook crossed herself and stepped out of their
way. As an afterthought, she pulled a juicy bone from

the stew pot and wrapped it in a napkin. 'In case you need it.'

Margaret nodded her thanks and they went into the garden. As they rounded the corner of the house, the kennel came in sight and an ageing pug let out what he probably thought was a fearsome battle cry, but was actually an endless series of wheezy barks. The sound carried surprisingly well in the walled garden and he suspected anyone near an open window in the house was thoroughly annoyed by it.

Suddenly, the little dog tired of idle threats and launched himself from his house, charging David with the confidence of a lion on an antelope. The dog did not go silent until his little teeth sank into the flesh of David's ankle.

David let out a string of curses that no lady should hear. Then he hissed through clenched teeth and gave Lady Margaret a pleading look. 'Get this monster off of me.'

In response, she smiled, obviously pleased that he had been paid back in some part for the tricks he had already played. She had warned him, and now he was getting what he deserved. 'Caesar,' she called, with no particular enthusiasm, 'stop it.'

The dog ignored her.

David gave a sharp kick of his leg to dislodge the animal and was free for only a moment before it snapped again, catching the leg of his pantaloons and worrying the fabric until it ripped.

'Caesar,' she said again, then unwrapped the bone and dropped it directly in front of him.

The dog immediately freed David's leg and tried to pick up the bone. Since it was bigger than his head, the best he could do was a slow, industrious drag back to his house, growling happily the whole way.

She looked back to David, as he rubbed his ankle and stared in dismay at his ripped pantaloons. 'Now you have met my sister's dog. Was that what you were expecting to find?'

'He has more than lived up to his reputation,' David said, reaching into his pocket for a handkerchief to bind his wounded ankle. 'Was this dog present in the house when your father was killed?'

'My sister was here and so was he,' she said. 'She would never leave him in the country. The servants there want no part of him.'

'And where is the window to the study?' he asked.

She stared back at the house and picked it out of the row of the windows, pointing.

'So, if someone attempted to break in from the yard, as the open window of the study implied, the dog would have barked to alert the house, then attacked him.' David paused, waiting to see if she could offer anything more than a denial of the obvious.

'I had not thought of that,' she admitted.

'The killer must have come into the study from inside the house,' he said.

'Or they might have known the house well enough to bring a bone to bribe the dog,' she said, pointing to where the pug lay, almost at their feet, oblivious to all but the treat from the kitchen.

'Perhaps,' he allowed. 'But even though you knew him, it still took some time to quiet him down. I find it odd that no one commented on the dog barking the night your father died. It seems more likely that they entered through the door of the study and knew your father well enough to get close to him so they might strike.'

Her brow furrowed, considering the possibilities. 'But that does not mean that it had to be Hugh,' she said at last. 'It might have been a servant, or a visitor Father invited to the house, who escaped in the confusion.'

'I am willing to consider any possibility,' he said. 'But someone must have seen a guest arrive and no one remarked on it when questioned by the Runners. I have already been told that there was an exodus of the staff after your father died. Perhaps a killer could have slipped away under the guise of being unwilling to serve your brother.'

'If I get you a list of the ones who left, will you investigate them?' she asked.

'It would be foolish of me not to,' he said.

This brought a smile to her face, as if she had already convinced herself that the answer lay somewhere in that group of people.

'I will have the names for you by your next visit,' she said. 'But now I think we should return to the music room before Olivia comes back into the garden and finds us on the wrong side of the window.'

As she led him back through the kitchen, the cook

cast a sympathetic look in the direction of his ankle
and slipped a warm biscuit from a plate on the table,
offering it to him without a word.

He nodded his thanks and took it, limping after
Lady Margaret as they made their way to the music
room. Once there, she shut the door behind them
and stared at him as he finished his biscuit, licking
the crumbs from his fingers. He could not resist re-
marking, 'I still do not like your brother, but the staff
here are very nice.'

'Because they do not know you as well as I do,'
she said, eying the biscuit crumbs with envy.

He gave her a pitiful look and glanced down at his
ankle. 'I am sure you will have multiple opportunities
to get me back, as we work together…because this
really will work better with your help. You may not
believe it, but I do value the truth above revenge. And
I value your safety above both of those. If, for some
reason, you feel the risk is too great and you cannot
continue to help me, you have but to tell me and it
will be as if it had never happened.' It was a half-
truth at best. He would not risk her life by turning
her brother against her. But there would be no way
to erase the doubts he might have raised in her by the
continual questioning of a man she clearly admired.

For a moment, her expression softened and she
looked at him as she had on his last visit, when she
had seen him as a man and not a threat. 'I want to
believe you,' she said. Then she smiled. 'It will be
easier to do so once I've proven you wrong.'

'Of course,' he agreed, smiling back at her and

feeling some of the easy camaraderie between them returning.

There was a whistle from the window, signifying the return of Lady Olivia and the end of the day's lesson.

Chapter Six

It had been a very confusing day.

Peg had gone from the wild optimism of waiting for her first real kiss to the crushing disappointment of learning David Castell's true mission. And from there, she had found a place somewhere in between, understanding his motives, but unsure whether she liked or trusted him.

He seemed genuinely concerned about her safety, just as he had on the first day. She could not help the warm, comforted feelings that rose when she thought of his promise to put her safety ahead of his desire for the truth. Since she was in no danger, the point was moot, but it was nice to hear, all the same.

There was also the fact that he seemed to grow more attractive each time she saw him. Now that he had given up pretending that he was a dancing master, it was easier to see the flashes of intelligence in his dark eyes. His smile, which had been cartoonishly broad at first, had settled into an expression that was warm and inviting and she could hardly resist smiling in response. Though his clothing was still ridiculously tight, it only encouraged her to admire his physique. And, as if he had known what she'd been thinking, he had forgone the hair oil he had used on his first visits, revealing a tangle of curls that made her fingers itch to touch them.

She squeezed her eyes shut tight, as if it was possible to hide from the images in her mind by shutting out the light of day. She had to remember that he might be handsome, but he was a handsome villain. It was a risk to her family to have such warm thoughts about an enemy. She must remember where her loyalties lied. Family came first. If not for them, she had nothing.

She needed wise counsel and she could certainly not ask Hugh what was to be done about the man. Her sister, however, was likely to offer advice whether she asked for it or not. She had returned from her visit with Alister with the same smug smile she had worn on the last few escapes. It was clear her version of their dancing lessons suited her well.

And now, as they took their afternoon tea in the sitting room, she was eager to hear that Peg's day had been just as satisfying. 'How goes it with your friend, Mr Castell?' she said, her smile hidden by her raised cup.

'He is not my friend,' Peg said quickly. 'At least, I do not think he is.'

'Then he has either taken too many liberties, or not enough,' Liv replied.

'We did not kiss today, if that is what you mean,' Peg said, surprised to feel lingering regret over the fact.

'No kisses.' Liv tutted in disapproval. 'Then tell me all. What has he done to displease you? Trod on your toes as you danced?'

'We did not dance, either,' Peg admitted. 'We talked.'

Liv rolled her eyes. 'You are never going to get anywhere until you stop doing that. What was the topic that upset you?'

'Mr Castell thinks that Hugh killed Father,' she blurted, relieved that it was finally out in the open. Then she laughed, to show how ridiculous she thought the whole thing was.

But Liv did not laugh in response. Nor did she offer the hasty denial that Peg had been expecting. Instead, she remained silent, as if waiting for more.

'And Hugh is not helping matters at all,' Peg added. 'He threatened to kill Mr Castell if he touched either of us.'

'Then it is a wonder you got the little kiss that you did,' Liv said. 'Mr Castell must be a very brave man.'

'You do not believe the rumours, do you?' Peg prompted, still waiting for her sister's denial.

But Liv's face was blank, showing none of the shock and outrage Peg had expected. 'I do not know what to believe,' Liv said at last. 'But it is the most logical answer, isn't it?'

'Logical?' Peg said, shocked. 'You are speaking of Hugh. Our brother,' she added, for emphasis.

'The Duke of Scofield is a different person from the boy we played with in the nursery,' Liv said gently.

'But still…' Peg shook her head '…you are talking about cold-blooded murder.'

'Hot-blooded, I should think,' Liv corrected. 'Do you remember how they used to argue when Father was alive? There were threats made on both sides.'

'But I did not think they were serious,' Peg said, stunned. 'Hugh learned to argue from Father who, though he was constantly wanting to kill someone or other, never did.'

'To the best of our knowledge,' her sister added.

'Surely we'd have heard something,' Peg said, embarrassed that she would even consider her father capable of violence. 'They were only words.'

'Loose talk is all well and good, until the body is found,' Liv reminded her. 'Then things are very different, indeed.'

'But do you think Hugh could have done such a thing? To his own father?' she asked, the last words in a whisper, as if saying them out loud might make them real.

'He was home when it happened,' Liv replied. 'He had the most to gain by Father's death. And I can think of no one else who might have done it.'

If what she said was true, Liv had not trusted their brother for two years, yet she had said nothing to indicate the fact. 'But that means that we are in the power of a murderer.'

'A murderer who is still our brother,' Liv reminded

her. 'If he is guilty, what are we to do about it? What action could we take that would not make matters far worse than they already are?'

Peg paused to consider and found that she was unable to give an answer. What her sister was saying sounded too much like what Mr Castell had said earlier.

When she did not respond, Liv continued. 'He is our guardian. If, for some reason, he would be prosecuted for a crime, what would become of us?'

It would be complete and utter ruin. They would be out in the street, with no other family to take them in.

'I suspect the rumours about him have done enough damage to our reputations,' Liv reminded her. 'It is a shame that Hugh will not give you a Season, since it would be the quickest way to reveal who is for us and who is against.'

'There is still that much ill feeling?' Peg said, shocked.

'We will not know for sure until we socialise, which is probably why Hugh will not allow it,' Liv replied. 'He is still a duke and that overcomes much. At least Alister is not overly bothered by the stories about him. But if they were to arrest him and take the title from him, I doubt even Alister's patience would hold. No one would have us then.'

'Hugh will not allow anyone to have us now,' Peg reminded her. 'We are as close to prisoners in this house as it is possible to be.'

'Because he does not want you talking to people

like Mr Castell, who will fill your head with unpleasant facts,' Liv added.

'Rumours,' Peg corrected. 'No one saw the crime happen. We cannot possibly be sure.'

'Perhaps we will never know the truth,' Liv agreed. 'But that does not change the mess we are in. When I marry Alister, I mean for you to come live with us. Once you are no longer under Hugh's control, we will find a proper suitor for you. We will get through this.' Liv reached out and gave her hand an encouraging squeeze.

'Hugh will not allow you to marry Alister,' Peg reminded her. 'He has already refused the offer.'

Liv took a deep breath, as if steadying her nerves. 'I am still trying to persuade him. But if he will not come around, there is always Gretna Green.' She said this with a resignation that held none of the excitement a romantic elopement should.

'Or you do not have to marry him at all,' Peg reminded her. 'If you do not want him, then wait for another suitor, or remain single.'

'But he has been waiting so patiently for me, it hardly seems fair to cast him off now,' Liv said with a smile. 'And it has been very exciting to carry on an illicit liaison. But sometimes I fear that things will be different when we do not need to sneak around and can express our love openly.'

'They will change for the better, I hope,' Peg said. 'If they do not, I will not allow you to marry him just to get me away from this house. I do not need you martyring yourself for my sake.'

'It is not martyrdom to marry a fine gentleman like Alister,' her sister insisted, though she still sounded too calculated to be a woman in the throes of passion. 'And if I do not help you, who will? It is not as if Hugh will allow you out of the house to meet any men on your own.'

'Perhaps he will change his mind, once you are married,' Peg replied. 'He will be used to the idea of losing his little sisters after one of us has gone. I suspect, once he thinks about it, he will be glad to get me off his hands.'

'We can hope,' Liv replied. 'I have no idea why he is so set against us marrying in the first place. I do not think it is just Alister he dislikes. When I speak to him, I get the distinct impression that no man is good enough for us.'

'If the rest of London is as convinced of his guilt as Mr Castell is, then I do not hold much hope of our chances. Beggars cannot be choosers, can they?'

She was trying to lighten the mood, but her sister gave a sombre nod in response to this. 'He may be trying to hide the fact by isolating us, but his infamy has ruined our reputations.'

When the conversation had begun, Peg had never expected that her sister's views would align so closely with those of Mr Castell. Was she really the only one who believed that Hugh might be innocent? 'Perhaps some facts will come to light that prove him guilt-less,' she said, all the more convinced that she would find something to exonerate him.

Liv shrugged in response, as if she could not even

pretend to consider the possibility. 'Anything is possible, I suppose. But whether you come to live with
me after marriage or not, when you come of age, you
would do well to stay as far away from our brother as
you are able. Associating with him will make your
future more difficult, not less.'

If Hugh was truly a murderer, the suggestion was
a good one. Yet, even if he was not, at what point did
loyalty to family yield to self-preservation? If Hugh
did not mean to see her properly married and out of
his house, she might have to leave on her own.

A thought occurred to her. 'Suppose he keeps us
close because he needs us?' she asked. 'This must
be hard for him, as well.'

'Since we've been grown, when has he ever given
a hint of brotherly affection?' Liv asked, disgusted.
'He treated us as an inconvenience long before Father
died. And since?' She shuddered. 'He has been so
distant as to seem a stranger to me and not a brother
at all.'

'Perhaps if you made an effort to talk to him,' Peg
said. But even she had to admit that the majority of
interactions she had with Hugh did not extend beyond companionable silence at breakfast.

Liv shook her head. 'I want to believe the best of
him, Peg. He is our brother, after all. But he does not
give me a reason to trust in him. You may play nice
with him and try to understand. I will continue as I
am doing and try to find a path out of this house for
the pair of us. If we do not find some way to separate
ourselves from Hugh, in the end, he will ruin us all.'

Chapter Seven

David received a list of the servants that had left the Scofield household in the afternoon post, sent care of the *Daily Standard* to him. But his plan to investigate them would be more difficult than he thought.

There were six names and he eliminated three of them immediately. The lady's maid the girls had shared was more likely spooked by a death in the house than strong enough to be a cold-blooded killer. Likewise, the youngest footman, who was barely fourteen when he'd run off, complaining of missing his mam. The butler who left used the excuse that he was old and ready to return to family in the north rather than accept a new master.

The remaining three names, two footmen and a groundskeeper, were all able-bodied, adult men, strong enough to strike the blow that had rendered them masterless. But when they had gone, they'd left no forwarding information and only the vaguest of plans to take positions elsewhere. Short of knocking on every back door in Britain, he was unsure how he would track them down.

Still, it was more information than he'd had about the staff at the time of the old Duke's murder and he stored it among the rest of his notes, hoping it would prove useful later.

The next day, when he visited the Scofield house to give his supposed dance lesson, Margaret and her sister were waiting for him in the music room. When she looked at him, his partner in crime showed no sign of eagerness for his presence or for the investigation to come. He felt a pang of regret for the innocent curiosity that had been lost in the last days and the smiles that she had given him before she'd known the truth.

Today, she said nothing, simply leading her sister to the window and all but pushing her out of it, so they could be alone. She turned back to him, hands on hips. 'What do you want to see today?'

'No second thoughts?' he asked, a little surprised by her resolute attitude.

'I have spoken to my sister about the matter,' she said, then held up a hand. 'Not the details of your plan, of course. But Olivia has left me feeling that the sooner that Hugh's innocence is established, the better.'

'I see,' he said, offering a silent prayer that, against all logic, he might be wrong. He had no idea what she might do if her hopes were dashed, but he did not want to be the blame for it.

'What do you want me to show you?' she prompted again, with a defiant set to her jaw that said she had no intention of turning back, no matter the risks.

'Let us go to your brother's room,' he said, not entirely surprised when her look of resolution turned to dismay.

'Do you really think anything will be there?' she said, obviously wishing that the answer might be 'no'.

'We will not know unless we look,' he reminded her.

'If the door is locked, I will not be able to open it,' she said.

'We will worry about that after we have tried it,' he said with a shrug, wondering if it would be unfair to ask her to steal a key.

But when they got to the door, it opened easily and Peg pulled him quickly into the room, shutting it behind them. 'There. Now look for what you want and let us be out of here before we are discovered.' She pressed her ear to the door, listening for servants in the hall.

He turned back to the room, looking for anything out of place. But apparently, the Duke was one of those annoying men who let his valet rule his life for there was not so much as a hair in the hairbrush to indicate that the room was used nightly. The linen in the drawers was meticulously folded and nothing hid beneath it. The wardrobe was full of pressed and brushed coats, vests and breeches, without as much as a handkerchief in any of the pockets. The writing desk by the window did not appear to have ever been used. The ink well was empty and the blotter clean.

'Are we finished?' Peg whispered from the doorway.

'Almost,' he said with a sigh, reaching for the last drawer in the bedside table. 'There is nothing...' Then he stopped, staring down at the token sitting in pride of place on a linen handkerchief. He looked to Margaret. 'Come here and tell me if you recognise this.'

She hurried across the room to him and stared down into the drawer. 'It is a lock of woman's hair,' she said, stating the obvious.

'But whose?' he asked.

She prodded it with her finger, taking care not to disarrange it. 'It does not belong to my sister or me, or to our mother. We are all blonde and this is such a fine auburn that I cannot imagine it is not natural.'

Nor did it match the red hair of the only woman he knew to be associated with Scofield. 'Did he have a childhood love? Has he ever offered for someone and been refused, or paid court to a special lady above all others?'

'Not that I know of,' Margaret said, her brow furrowed. 'I cannot say that my brother lives the life of a monk. But neither has he told me of anyone special, in all the time I've known him.' She stared down at the lock, which was bound at the end with a bit of blue string and curled tightly enough to fit in the back of a pocket watch, should a gentleman choose to carry it there.

'It is very romantic,' she said, at last.

'I suppose it is,' he said, stealing a glance at the honey curls brushing her shoulders and imagining what a similar token might mean to the bearer.

'It supports my version of events, more than yours,' she said, stroking it very gently with a finger.

'Why would you think so?' he said, confused.

'The version of my brother that you present is a man driven by anger to commit violent acts,' she said. 'To me, that does not fit with a man who would cherish a keepsake or obsess over a lost love when in private.'

'His argument with Dick Sterling was over a woman,' David countered.

'And this is not her hair,' Margaret said, shaking her head. 'You'd have recognised it otherwise and pointed it out to me as proof for your side.'

'Probably true,' he replied, surprised at the astuteness of her reasoning.

'And I defy you to come up with the story of an auburn-haired lady, tragically murdered, that you can blame on my brother,' she said. 'Even I would have noticed such a story in the paper and remarked on it.'

Looking back over several years, he could not think of any, nor had there been a mysterious death among the ladybirds favoured by the aristocracy.

'My brother, a man who you are convinced is so dangerous that he might do harm to me and Olivia, hides in his room and pines over a token from a woman he cannot have,' she said, with the sort of devilish smile that a younger sister might have when she had found a delicious piece of gossip that she had no idea how to use. She glanced up at David, her eyes sparkling with mirth. 'I must say, this opens an interesting window on his character for me and I know him better than any other person. Except her, perhaps,' she said, touching the lock of hair again.

His heart beat quicker as well, for this was a possibility he never would have considered. Somewhere in England, there was a woman who knew hidden truths about Scofield that his family did not. 'She might be dead,' David said, not wanting to leave a possibility unconsidered.

'Oh, no. I do not think so,' Margaret replied.

'How can you be sure?' he asked.

'Because, though it is necessary for a duke to marry and get an heir for succession, he has made no effort to find a wife. For some reason, he cannot have the woman he wants. If he is still holding out hope, she is likely alive and single.'

He stared at her, fascinated. 'It is all surmise. And yet...'

'Your theories have no more basis in fact than mine,' she reminded him.

He grinned at her. 'But yours give me much to consider. There is a woman out there, somewhere, who may have all the answers to our questions.'

She smiled back at him and, for a moment, he felt a flash of the connection that had linked them before she had found out who he really was. 'Perhaps, with my help, you will be able to find her.'

'Perhaps so. We work well together,' he said, not wanting to lose the feeling.

She nodded. 'You are already considering possibilities that you might have rejected before. It is proof that you need me to help you find the truth. I am opening your mind.'

A part of him wanted to argue that there had been nothing wrong with his mind before he had met her. A single lock of hair did not mean her brother was an innocent man. But he was enjoying the easy companionship between them too much to spoil it with an argument. He glanced back at the keepsake to make sure it looked as it had when they found it, then slid the drawer shut. 'I think that is all we will find here,' he said. 'We should go before we are discovered.'

She nodded again and hurried to the door, opening it a crack and sticking her head into the hall. When she was sure the way was clear, she gestured him forward, pushing him past her so she could close the door. 'I hope you did not move anything. Hugh might not notice, but his valet surely will.'

'I was very careful,' he assured her.

In front of them, he heard the sound of light footsteps running up the main stairs. Before he could think, Margaret had grabbed him by the arm and dragged him into the nearest bedroom, shutting the door behind them.

'Where are we?' he whispered.

'My room,' she said.

He started. 'I cannot be found here.'

'You cannot be found anywhere above stairs,' she

said, exasperated. 'But at least, if you are found here, I can come up with a logical explanation for it.'

The most logical explanation was one that was likely to get him killed. 'I would much rather that your brother thought I was rummaging through his linen than yours.'

She laughed softly. 'I promise not to tell him that you were in my room.'

Her hand was still resting on his arm from when she had pulled him into her room. Such a gentle touch should not be having such an effect on him, but it seemed to freeze him in place, standing too close to her to be proper. Afraid to look her in the eyes, he glanced behind them and saw an attractively decorated room with a very large bed, hung with blue velvet curtains. It seemed to be an awful lot of space for just one small girl. It made him wonder how nicely two might share it.

He turned quickly back to look at her, facing his earlier fear. She was just as pretty as she had been the first time he had seen her and smiling up at him as if they were caught in a shared joke. But though they had spent much of their time together unchaperoned, it had never felt as dangerous as this did, with a bed near and the two of them standing closer than they had ever done. His mind seemed to cloud and time slowed until each moment was an eternity full of delicious tension.

She noticed the change in him and her smile faded, but she did not draw away. Instead, she closed her eyes, leaned towards him and waited.

The opportunity was too good to resist. He dropped his head and kissed her on the mouth, as he had wanted to from the first moment he'd met her. In response, she sighed and snuggled against him, putting her arms tentatively around his waist. He put his hands on her shoulders, steadying her and himself. In a way, it was like dancing, but he must remember that she was not supposed to be the one to lead. He had promised her the perfect first kiss. It was up to him to provide it.

He took his time with her, making sure his lips were firm but gentle. He teased her mouth, tasting each inch of it, and touching the bow with the tip of his tongue, slowly running it along the closed crease of her lips, only to retreat when she opened them in invitation. Then, he began again, savouring the sigh of frustration that escaped as he retreated.

The fact that something was wrong cut through the passion-soaked haze in his brain before he could identify the nature of the problem. The room had been silent when they'd entered, but now there were sounds of movement coming from somewhere behind them. They were about to be discovered.

He tried to withdraw so they might compose themselves, but before he could release her Margaret had latched on even tighter, forcing her lips against his with the awkwardness of an overeager virgin. He struggled to free himself, but she clung to him like ivy on a stone fence.

In the midst of their battle, the door to the dressing room opened. When he had managed to thrash himself clear of the lovely arms that bound him, he saw a lady's maid giggling in the doorway, the linen she had been carrying dropped in a heap at her feet. She smothered the laugh with a hand and hurried to pick up after herself, giving them a moment to regroup. By the time she looked up at them again, they were standing a respectable distance apart, trying and failing to pretend that nothing had happened.

'I did not mean to interrupt, my lady,' she said, focusing carefully on her mistress and doing her best to pretend that there was not another person in the room with them. 'You are not usually in your bedroom at this hour. I did not expect...'

'Of course you did not, Jenny,' Margaret said, smoothing her skirts and giving the girl a tight smile. 'And I would hope that you will not tell anyone that you saw me here today.'

The girl glanced quickly from Margaret to David and back again, and then said, 'Of course not, my lady. I did not see anything.'

'Thank you,' Margaret said, obviously relieved. 'And now, I think we can...um...continue our tour of the house, Mr Castellano.'

'Of course,' he said, forcing a brilliant smile on the maid and trying to act as if nothing had happened.

Then Margaret spoiled the pretended innocence of the moment by asking, 'Did you happen to see anyone in the main hall when you were on your way to this room?'

'No, my lady,' the maid said. 'The way is clear.'

'Very good.' She grabbed David by the arm and hauled him from her room, hurrying for the stairs.

They were silent until they were safely shut up in the music room again, then she seemed to collapse in upon herself, breathing heavily as if they had run the whole way down the stairs.

He was not much better. 'You kissed me,' he said, still shocked by the crash of her teeth against his, the thrust of her tongue in his mouth and her arms, locked about him in a death grip.

'You kissed me first,' she reminded him, pressing her hands to her cheeks as if trying to force the colour from them.

'I am aware of that,' he admitted, embarrassed. 'But when we were about to be discovered, you could have stepped away. Instead, you made the situation worse rather than better.'

'I made the situation different,' she said, giving him a knowing look. 'It was far more dangerous for you than for me. I wanted to even the odds.'

'But your reputation…'

'Will be undamaged by anyone in this house,' she said. 'The servants are not about to spread it through town that there was a man in my room. The worst that will happen is that they will tell my sister. But when they do, she will hear that I attacked you.'

'That is your plan?' he said doubtfully.

'When Jenny entered the room, you appeared to be fighting for your life. When you did get away from me, you looked as if you had been mauled by a wild beast. The expression on your face was quite comical,' she added with a smile.

'I am sure it was not that bad,' he said, trying not to think of the abject failure his first attempt at awakening her passions had been.

'On the contrary, it could not have gone better if we had planned it in advance,' she said. 'And you must admit, what we found in Hugh's room was exceptionally interesting.'

'Interesting? Yes. But I cannot say that it makes me believe he is innocent.'

She looked crestfallen for a moment, then her smile returned. 'There are still places for us to search and questions to be asked. We have only just begun.'

'That is very true,' he said. But when he looked at her, he had a hard time remembering his true purpose. He could only think of the kiss and what a delightful beginning that might be. Since he could not control his foolish thoughts, it was probably fortunate for both of them that Olivia whistled from the garden, signalling an end to their time together.

Chapter Eight

She had been given her first proper kiss, and it had been everything she had hoped for. It had not ended well, of course. But it was probably for the best that Jenny had interrupted them. Peg had had no idea how things might have ended, otherwise.

She had always assumed that only girls of weak character would be willing to throw away their virtue on a dishonourable man. But it had taken just one kiss to see how the temptation to do so might be irresistible.

The kiss she had given him in return had been purposely awkward and embarrassing for everyone concerned. But it had spared her from revealing her true feelings, which were quite different than she wished them to be.

No matter how many times she reminded herself that David Castell was a liar, a manipulator and a danger to her family, she could not seem to overcome the fact that she liked him. He seemed to grow more interesting with each visit and remained solicitous of her, despite what he felt for Hugh.

He was also a good kisser.

It was the last thing she should be focusing on. Yet she had not been able to sleep for reliving the moment that his lips had touched hers. The fact that it had happened in her bedroom made it even more difficult to rest easy. She could not stop trying to imagine what might have happened, had they not been interrupted.

The next morning, at breakfast, she abandoned her usual chocolate in favour of a cup of strong coffee, yawning into her hand as she poured it.

Fortunately, Hugh was too absorbed in the post he was reading to give her much notice. Since he would not pay attention to her, she took the opportunity to observe him, wondering what it was that people saw that convinced them he was capable of murder. To her, he still looked like the same distant older brother he had always been.

'Hugh,' she said, buttering a muffin and trying to be casual.

'Whatever it is, the answer is no,' he said, not looking up from his letter.

'You do not even know what I am about to say,' she said.

'But I doubt that will change my answer,' he said, setting the letter down beside his plate and looking at her. 'What do you want now?'

'Nothing,' she assured him. 'But I was wondering. Since you are not ready to see either Olivia or I married…'

'We have been over that ground before,' he said with a sigh.

She held up a hand to stop him. 'Is there any chance that you will be marrying soon? You should be seeing to the succession, after all.'

'Me?' It was clear from his tone that this was the last question he had expected to hear from her. He paused for a moment, as if he had no idea how to answer. Then he replied, 'Certainly not,' and reached for the rest of his mail, eager to avoid further conversation.

Before he could shut her out, she said, 'But you do need an heir. You will have to marry at some point.'

'The thought had occurred to me,' he replied, and she was surprised to see a flash of something in his eyes that looked almost like pain. 'But there are some things that even obligation to the Crown cannot make me do. I do not plan to marry. Not soon. Not ever.' He went back to his post, breaking the seal on the next letter to make it clear that he would be taking no more questions from her.

This was interesting. Though he would not admit to having a tragic, lost love, this complete refusal to marry was closer to a confirmation of her suspicions than she had thought to get. What could there be to put him so far off the marital sacrament that he would eschew it now and for ever?

But how was she to find the identity of the one he was pining for? Since he was a gentleman, he would be far too polite to give her the name of the girl, if she pressed for it. She could think of only two other options. She could casually mention every single woman in London until she got a response, or she could ask Olivia if she remembered anything. She doubted either of them would succeed, but she meant to keep digging, for sisterly curiosity if nothing else.

Later in the day, while they were waiting in the music room for the arrival of David Castell and Olivia's inevitable escape, Peg took the opportunity to question her. 'Are things going well with Alister?' she said, to distract Liv from staring out the window.

'As well as they ever do,' she said with a pensive smile. 'It would be better if Hugh were more flexible, of course.'

'I asked him today at breakfast if he ever intends to marry, himself. He said no.'

Liv's head snapped around to pay full attention. 'But, of all of us, it is most important for him to do so.'

'I know,' Peg replied. 'But he is adamant. For a moment, he seemed almost like a man with a broken heart.'

Liv's response to this was to laugh out loud. 'I did not think Hugh had a heart at all, much less one that could be broken.'

'All the same, he behaved most strangely when I asked him about marriage. Do you think it is possible that he might be longing for a woman he cannot have?'

'Anything is possible,' Liv replied. 'But I cannot think who she might be. I have never seen him pay particular attention to any girl back when Father was alive and we were both going about in society.'

'Perhaps she was inappropriate in some way,' Peg said, allowing herself a delicious shiver at the thought. Perhaps he might sympathise with an attraction outside one's social class if he had already experienced one.

Liv had put a fingertip to her lips, considering. 'I can think of only one unusual thing I have caught him doing and that was ages ago, before Father died.'

'What was that?'

'I came into the morning room and caught him writing a letter.'

'Not so strange,' Peg said, disappointed.

'It was his reaction on discovery that made it so,' Liv said. 'He turned bright red and spilled the inkwell in his rush to hide what he was doing from me. I have never seen him so embarrassed, before or since.'

'Do you think it was a *billet doux*?' she said, her earlier concerns about the murder overshadowed by this delicious bit of gossip.

'I cannot think what else it might have been,' Liv replied, grinning back at her.

'Then he was in love, once,' Peg said.

'And may still be, if he does not plan to marry,' Liv said in triumph. 'Perhaps our big brother is human, after all.'

'More than we know,' Peg assured her, thinking

of the lock of hair and the thrill of forbidden love, and equally forbidden kisses.

Just then, Mr Castell appeared in the doorway, ready for the day's pretend dancing lesson.

'Right,' Liv said, forgetting all about the conversation they'd been having. 'I'm off.'

When Peg had finished helping her out of the window, she turned back to greet him. 'Hugh is still in love with someone he met before Father died.'

'Interesting,' he said. But by the bland look he gave her, Mr Castell was not as impressed as he should have been.

'I know it does not prove him innocent,' she said hurriedly. 'But it does prove that he is not the murderous automaton that you made him out to be.'

'Not an automaton,' he agreed with a sympathetic tilt of his head. 'But we will have to find something better than that to convince me that he is innocent.'

'Where do you wish to search today?' she said. 'Not above stairs, I hope.'

He smiled at her. 'I am afraid I cannot trust you with my virtue if we stray too close to the bedrooms.'

She smiled back at him to share the joke. But a part of her regretted that they had decided the interlude in the bedroom was a source of amusement and not something that might be repeated. 'No more bedrooms,' she agreed. 'The study?'

'I was thinking of just the place,' he said. 'Has your brother left the house?'

'Just after breakfast,' she said, walking to the door of the music room and opening it. When she was sure that the hall was empty, she led him to the study, shutting the door quickly behind them. 'Here you are. What do you mean to do with the time?'

He looked around him, hesitating, as if he was not quite sure where to begin. She could not blame him, for her brother's presence seemed to linger in this room, as if he had never left it.

'Come on, then,' she said, to bully him to action. 'It is not as if you are going to find a written confession sitting on the desk.'

In response to her urging, he reached for a desk drawer and gave a futile tug that rattled the lock.

She smiled at his look of frustration and walked to the desk, removing a pin from her hair as she went. She checked each drawer in turn, picking locks and leaving them open for his inspection. Once she was done, she stepped away and gestured for him to search.

'How did a duke's daughter learn to do that?' he said, his reverie broken.

'My father was in the habit of keeping boiled sweets in the bottom drawer,' she said with a smile. 'It did not take him long to realise that I stole from him and it took me even less to learn to pick the lock when he tried to keep me out of them.' She glanced down at the desk. 'I will put everything back to the way it was once you have had a look at the contents.' She stepped away from the desk and stationed herself by the door to listen for interruptions.

He walked around the desk and began to examine the contents, taking care not to disturb the arrangement of the items therein. She could see from where she stood that much of it was uninteresting: extra quills, a dried-out bottle of ink, a stack of receipts. It was a disappointing collection, reminiscent of the things that had been in the desk when it had belonged to her father.

Then he pulled a stack of journals from the bottom drawer. He smiled up at her and tapped them with his finger. 'This is exactly the window into the mind of the Duke that I have been hoping to find. And I could not have done it without you.' He dropped into her brother's desk chair, as if he belonged there, grabbed the top diary and paged backwards, scanning the entries.

It was then that the enormity of what she was doing struck her. She had been so sure that Hugh was innocent she had never thought of what might happen if she was wrong. She might have led a stranger directly to the thing that would ruin them all.

'Damn.' The single word was said in a normal tone, but it seemed overloud in the quiet of the study.

'What did you find?' she said, hurrying to his side.

'Nothing,' he said, rippling through the pages. 'Nothing interesting, at least. The evening that Richard Sterling died, he writes that he dined at his club, lost several pounds playing whist, came home and retired early.'

David paged forward several pages, so agitated that the paper nearly tore beneath his fingers. 'There is not even a mention that the body had been discovered. It is as if the death did not matter to him in the slightest.'

'Perhaps it did not,' Peg said gently. 'Were Hugh and this Mr Sterling close friends?'

'Not as far as I knew,' David admitted. 'Scofield was doing his best to make an enemy of him.'

'So, my brother was rude, dismissive and threatening,' Peg said. 'Just as he is to everyone else.'

'They argued,' he insisted. 'There were many witnesses to it.'

'Just as I witnessed Hugh arguing with Father on the night he died,' Peg agreed. 'But that does not prove he killed him. What was the topic of his argument with Mr Sterling?'

'It was a subject not fit for a lady's ears,' he said, sounding embarrassingly prim. Apparently, there were a few secrets he was unwilling to share with her. At least, not yet.

'How do you expect me to help if you will not tell me what happened?' she asked.

He sighed. 'They were arguing over a woman.' He paged back through the journal. 'There is a brief mention of it here and a line or two about the argument, but nothing in the writing indicates that it was important.'

'It is just as I told you,' she said. 'Despite what he might say in public, in private his feelings are quite different.'

'Or he is lying in his journal to make things seem less important than they are,' Mr Castell countered.

'So, you are not satisfied that my brother had nothing to do with the death of your friend,' she said, leaning over his shoulder to try to read the entry about the argument.

'No,' he admitted, shutting the book before she could see.

'But you found nothing in this book to support your theory,' she reminded him.

'That is not the only murder we must concern ourselves with,' he countered, rummaging through the drawer for another volume, flipping pages and checking dates. 'Let us see what he has to say about your father's death, shall we?'

She drew back, uncomfortably aware of the violation she committed in searching her brother's most intimate secrets and the fact that what they might find in this book could break her heart.

He turned the pages slower now, looking for the correct entries. But when he arrived at the date of the murder, he held out the book to show what he had found. All that was left of the entry were ragged scraps where the pertinent pages had been ripped from the book. On the next page, a single line had been written:

Oh, God, what am I to do now?

Now he was staring at her, waiting to see her reaction.

It was hard to come up with one while she was imagining her brother, in a fit of panic, scribbling an entry only to rip it from the book and throw it into the fire. 'We cannot truly know what this means, without the missing pages,' she said, more to her-self than to him.

'But it does not look good,' he reminded her. He was trying to be gentle, but she could detect a note of triumph in his voice.

She stared at the line that remained. 'Surely, if he had just committed a murder, he would have said, "What have I done?" not "What am I to do?"'

He thought for a moment. 'That is an interest-ing take on the words written, but I am not sure it is significant. People are careless when they are under stress, as your brother clearly was.'

'But we cannot know what he was thinking from a single sentence.'

He flicked a finger over what was left of the torn pages. 'But we can see that he wrote something and decided that it was too dangerous to survive, even in a private journal.'

'It was a difficult time for all of us,' she said, shaking her head.

'And yet I do not think you have a diary in your room with missing pages and cryptic statements.'

Of course, she did not. At the time, she had been encouraged not to think about the crime at all, much less speak or write of it, lest it be too upsetting to her delicate, girlish sensibilities. Her sister had been told the same. They had gone through the motions of the funeral as if it were a show and displayed all the expected behaviours of grief and mourning. But the family had never discussed what had happened at all. 'We are really not the sort of people to dwell on misfortune,' she said at last. 'There is a certain decorum to be maintained…'

He was staring at her as if she was speaking a foreign language. Perhaps she was. The words coming out of her mouth sounded like something Hugh might say when he wanted her to be quiet and do as she was told.

At last he said, 'I think we have seen all we can here. Let us put the desk to rights and go back to the music room before your sister returns.'

He put the books back in the desk drawer in the order he'd found them and gestured to her to lock the drawers again.

She pulled out her hairpin and made quick work of the locks, then went to the door and checked the hall before leading him back to the place they were supposed to be. Once there, with the door properly shut against eavesdroppers, she turned to him and said, 'Today's search was interesting, but not conclusive. Where will we be looking in the future?'

If she truly cared for Hugh, she should not be embracing this investigation with such enthusiasm. Or was it the investigator that attracted her? Her heart kicked up at the thought of more exploration and she was eager to hear his next suggestion.

He sighed. 'I think that the rooms we have searched so far are all that will be necessary, in this house.'

She blinked. Surprised. Was it all over, as quick as this? 'You have nothing else you want to see here?'

'Unless you can think of something you want to show me,' he said.

He must see, by the blank look on her face, that she had no other ideas. Guilty or innocent, her brother was not such a fool as to keep incriminating information in the common rooms where his snooping sisters were likely to find it.

Still, there must be some good news in this. 'Does that mean that your investigation is ended?' she said. 'Since you have not found anything conclusive, will you leave Hugh in peace?'

'Since I do not have the answers I want, my investigation is nowhere near finished.' He reached out to take her hand. 'It is only your part in it that is coming to an end.'

She snatched her hand away, hurt that this sweet gesture was merely his way of saying goodbye. 'After all that has happened, you mean to leave me behind?' It was unfair of her to complain. They had known each other only a few days. But the time they'd spent together felt much longer and more intimate.

'I do not want to leave you,' he replied, a look of surprise on his face as if he had not planned to admit any such thing. 'But there are places that I mean to go that young ladies should not follow.'

'And things I cannot know, like the details of the argument between my brother and your friend,' she said, exasperated. 'Yet you have no trouble telling me that you think my brother is a murderer. Let us ignore the strictures of society for a moment. What other truth could be worse than that?'

He winced. 'There is so much wrong in this that I hardly know how to answer. Despite the scandal, you are a lady from one of the greatest families in England. I should not have involved you in any of this. I should not even be speaking to you, much less considering...' He stopped himself, as if unwilling to admit what he was thinking.

She pressed her advantage. 'If you are right and my brother is dangerous, surely anywhere you take me will be safer than leaving me here. And I could continue to provide some much-needed objectivity.'

'You mean you would argue with me on every point,' he said and could not help smiling.

'Someone must,' she reminded him. 'Your mind was made up long before you began this search. The courts do not presume guilt and neither should you.'

'I am not as unreasonably biased as you make me sound,' he insisted, but added nothing to support the claim.

'You will have to prove that to me,' she replied. 'And if you mean to give up the pretence of dance lessons, I will never see you again.' There was the real problem, out loud and in the open. Though he might think he had got all that was useful out of her, she was not ready to let him go.

She watched the struggle on his face, pleased to see that he was no more eager to part from her than she was from him. 'I will find a way,' he said at last. 'I am not quite sure where I will be taking you, or how we will get there. But you are right, you have been of help so far and could continue to be so.'

'You will not regret it,' she said. Then she remembered her sister's warning that taking too much was getting her nowhere. So, she took a step towards him, arms outstretched, eyes closed.

Apparently, the offer was too tempting to resist. He met her halfway, enfolding her in an embrace and finding her lips with his. It was as delightful as it had been in her room and, in some ways, even more dangerous. Here, they did not have to worry about discovery for the duration of the lesson. They had time and he was using it well, taking the liberty of exploring her mouth with his tongue.

She accepted him with a sigh, relaxing in his arms and rubbing against his body until her breasts were pressed tight against his chest, feeling them tingle despite the many layers of fabric that protected her.

As if he understood, he slipped a hand between them, running a finger through the delicate chiffon ruffles that rose all the way to her throat, guarding her skin from the touch of his lips. He traced the outline of her body with his fingertip, drawing a line from throat to belly, making her imagine the delights that freedom from this house might offer.

He sighed and ended the kiss, setting her gently back on her feet with an apologetic shake of his head. He touched the tip of her nose lightly with the tip of his finger and pushed her back several inches to put a safe distance between them. 'Lady Margaret, we must stop indulging ourselves before something truly inappropriate happens.'

'Please,' she said with a smile, 'no more honorifics. Call me Margaret. Better yet, call me Peg, as my friends do.'

'That is all you have got from my warning?' he said, lifting his eyes to heaven.

'And may I call you David?' she added, ignoring his warning. 'We have kissed several times now. It seems a shame to be so formal when we are alone.'

'Instead of Mr Castell,' he reminded her. 'Not Lord Castell. Like your normal acquaintance would be named.'

'I am aware of that, David,' she said, taking the liberty on herself since he had refused to offer it.

'And I am not even a proper mister,' he admitted. 'I am a bastard son. Though my father has acknowledged me and seen to my education, I will never be more than what I am now.'

'I do not think a title is the most important thing about a man,' she said. 'In fact, I have given it very little thought, up to this point.'

'That is because everyone, including you, has been assuming you will marry a gentleman with either wealth or power or family, or all of the above,' he reminded her.

'My brother would say that I should not consider marriage at all,' she said, surprised that the conversation had taken this turn after only a few kisses.

'Your brother also said he would kill me for what I have done so far,' David reminded her.

'And as I keep assuring you, once you get to know him, you will find you have nothing to fear.'

He laughed. 'No matter what happens, I doubt

the time will ever come when I "get to know" your brother.'

'That is probably true,' she said, feeling strangely sad over the fact. He must think her terribly foolish to have said such a thing. It proved how little she knew about the normal course of flirtations, which were supposed to end long before anything got serious.

But a part of her mind was wondering what would happen if David and Hugh did talk. Would they be able to overcome their mutual loathing? And since her brother seemed to hate all men that took interest in his sisters, was there anything that David could say that would make him seem like a worthy suitor?

She shook her head and shrugged, remembering her sister's advice to take advantage of the situation that had been presented to her. Whatever happened between her and David Castell was a transient event. She must enjoy it while she could for she doubted Hugh would allow her another chance like this one. 'But at the moment, I do not want to think about my brother,' she said, holding out her arms for another kiss.

He shook his head and stepped away. 'This is all wrong,' he reminded her. 'You should not be encouraging further familiarity between us. You should call down the servants and have me banned from the house for doing something as totally inappropriate as kissing you.'

She smiled back at him. 'Dancing masters are supposed to be somewhat inappropriate, aren't they? If not, there would be no reason to warn young girls against them.'

'I am not actually a dancing master,' he replied. 'I am something far worse. A ne'er-do-well with aspirations beyond my station.'

'That makes you even more interesting than a dancing master,' she said, smiling.

His face darkened. 'Is that what I am to you, some kind of novelty?'

'That is not what I meant,' she said hurriedly, not entirely sure what had angered him.

He responded with a bitter smile, 'Then you are too naive to know your own mind. Let us be honest with each other. These interludes have an extra appeal to you because you know your brother would disapprove of your choice. You have no real concern what might happen to me if we are discovered, because you cannot think any further ahead than the moment's pleasure.'

'I am sorry,' she said, still stunned at how quickly things had changed between them.

'I have to go,' he muttered, running a hand through his hair and glancing towards the door as if he wanted to be anywhere in the world but with her.

Just then, Liv whistled from the garden, giving Peg a reason to escape the awkwardness between them. When she got to the window she turned back, but David refused to meet her gaze. 'Until our next lesson, Mr Castell,' she said, willing him to understand that she had not meant to hurt him.

'My lady,' he said, blank-faced, bowing as if they were nothing more than student and teacher. Then he was gone.

* * *

David walked down the street, away from the town house, cursing under his breath. He had wanted to impress the woman with his skill as a lover. Then, he had behaved like an injured virgin who had given herself cheaply to someone who had no honourable plans for the future. What had he been thinking to raise such a fuss over her perfectly sensible admission? He had got as far as he had with her because she enjoyed getting forbidden kisses from an even more forbidden sort of man.

In turn, he had taken extra pleasure in kissing a woman he could not have. He had known, from the first, that his acquaintance with her would be temporary. Once he had got what he needed from her, he would be gone.

But one moment they had been talking about him getting to know her brother, and the next? It had been as if a door had slammed in his face. And before that, he had been kissing her and having feelings that did not feel the least bit temporary. And before that had happened, he had been trying to leave her for ever, to continue his investigation of Scofield outside the house.

It was as if there was a war going on inside him, between what he wanted and what he knew he was entitled to. Perhaps it was because he'd had no real family, but for most of his life he had been satisfied to live and work alone. Why did he suddenly feel the need for a partner in both? And why, of all women, did it have to be Peg Bethune?

He did his best to put her out of his mind, focusing on what he had found in the journals. As far as he was concerned, Scofield's entry after his father's death, or the lack of it, exonerated the servants that had left the family's service. If one of them had run mad with a knife, Scofield would have taken immediate action and had no trouble writing about it after. Nor would he have ripped out the pages that recorded the details. Whatever had happened, the Duke knew the truth of it and had taken pains to hide it from anyone smart enough to search for it.

But it was strange that there had been no serious mention of Dick Sterling in the later entries. If the killer was the Duke of Scofield, as he suspected, the man had grown much more cagey by his second murder. This time, he had been careful to reveal nothing in his writings to link him to the death. The absence was almost stranger than a confession. It was as if the argument with Sterling had made no impression on him at all.

It made sense if Peg was right and the Duke's wild threats had no real weight behind them. Perhaps he forgot what he said as soon as the words were out of his mouth. She was so adamant that it made David want to believe as well, just as he wanted to believe that she might feel real affection for him in spite of his deficiencies in rank.

He had never met a woman so optimistic. She kept her faith, even in the face of scathing public opinion and worrisome circumstantial evidence. She believed in her brother because she believed she knew his heart.

It was a shame that such devotion was wasted on Scofield, who did not seem to appreciate the loyalty he was shown. If only she could believe in David as she did her brother, he would not waste the gift he was given. He could move the world for her if she believed in him, or at least change it enough so they might be together for ever.

Chapter Nine

That afternoon, Peg was walking down the hall towards the library, daydreaming about sweet kisses and a man who seemed to grow both more exciting and more confusing with each visit. She had insulted him without meaning to, probably because she was so inexperienced that she could not even flirt correctly.

She should not have responded as she had when he'd called himself a ne'er-do-well. Instead, she should have chided him for speaking ill of himself. It appeared that he had come far with a minimum of help from his family, which was an indication of good character. She could not blame him for aspiring above his station when he had managed to get where he was living by his wits. It was not as if a title had fallen into his lap, as it had for her brother.

All in all, there was much that she admired about David Castell. It hurt to think he had left her convinced that she was a shallow, silly girl who would toy with his affection for the novelty of associating with someone from a lower class. Perhaps this was nothing more than a flirtation, but that did not mean she had any less respect for him, or would not consider an offer, should one be forthcoming.

Of course, the final decision on marriage did not lie with her. If David did offer, Hugh would refuse. Her lover's rank would not matter as much as the fact that he'd had the temerity to ask at all. It might help that David held her brother in contempt, as well. If he wanted her, he would not care what Hugh said.

But she did. Her loyalty had to lie with family, before all others. Hugh was her guardian and she had been brought up to be obedient. If pressed, she would obey him, even if his decision seemed irrational. Then she would be left just as Liv was, unable to settle for an elopement and waiting for a marriage that might never come.

She closed her eyes and sighed, reminding herself that it was foolish to worry about things that might never happen. She must take things as they came and the first step was to make sure David saw the errors in his logic and realised that there was nothing to write about. When that happened, she would see if his feelings for her were deep enough to last beyond a few stolen kisses. Only then did she need to think about Hugh's opinions of her suitor.

Suddenly, there was a patter of hurried steps on the rug behind her and a hand closed on her elbow. 'I need to talk to you about the dancing master,' Liv said in a whisper, pulling her down the hall and into the empty sitting room.

'There is no reason to be so dramatic about it,' Peg said, refusing to lower her voice.

'On the contrary, I think there is.' Liv looked both ways before shutting the door and then out the window to be sure no one was listening there. 'You have been seen creeping about the upstairs with him.'

Peg silently cursed Jenny, the maid, for revealing what she had promised to keep secret. Lord knew how many in the household must have heard about it if it had got back to Liv. 'Whatever you think of it, it is not as it appears,' she said with a smile.

'That hardly signifies,' her sister said. 'It is what other people think that matters. And it is assumed that your flirtation is getting far out of hand.'

'My flirtation?' She tried her best at an airy laugh. 'I am not having one of those. And might I remind you, you were the one encouraging me in that direction in the first place.'

'I meant a few kisses only,' her sister said in a ridiculously prim voice. 'Nothing that would be as harmful to your reputation as taking the man to your bed.'

'It was my bedroom,' she corrected. 'A room with a bed in it, which we did not use. We were only there to keep from being found elsewhere. Mr Castell wished to search the house.'

Her sister rolled her eyes. 'And what business does he have in the family rooms?'

'He is a newspaper reporter,' Peg said, with a sigh of relief at being able to share the truth. 'He is investigating Hugh. I am trying to prove to him that he has no reason to do so.'

'You are helping him?' Liv said, appalled.

'Only because it is the quickest way to clear up these terrible untruths,' Peg responded. 'He will get in far less trouble if someone from the family helps him than if we let him root around on his own, making unsupported assumptions.'

'And how is that going, so far?' Liv asked, with a raised eyebrow.

'Our investigation is in its formative stages,' she allowed.

'Not well, then,' Liv concluded.

'These things take time,' Peg countered. It did not sound as confident as she'd have liked.

'I imagine they do,' Liv said sceptically. 'And you do not mind that a bit, do you?'

'What are you implying?' Peg said, trying to sound indignant rather than guilty.

'That you are falling in love with a man who means to ruin us all,' Liv snapped. 'How can you be so foolish as to allow him to use you in this way?'

'He is not using me,' Peg said, hurt. Perhaps it had begun that way, but now he was accusing her of using him. She needed more time to figure out just what was going on between them.

'He has known you for only a few days and he already has you leading him around the house, searching our personal possessions,' her sister said, disgusted.

'Not ours,' Peg said. 'Just Hugh's.'

Liv sighed. 'I do not always like our brother, but that does not mean I wish to spy on him or allow others to do so.'

'Are you afraid of what he will find?' Peg snapped and realised from the awkward silence that followed that her surmise was likely true.

'It does not matter what he uncovers,' Liv said, stubbornly. 'He should not be doing it. I have a good mind to tell Hugh what you have been up to, so he can put a stop to it.'

'And then I will tell him what you are doing with your dancing time,' Peg said, triumphant to realise that she had a way to control the conversation.

Liv sucked on her lip, as if considering whether it would be worth the risk.

'You know Hugh will never allow you to see Alister again if he discovers you have been sneaking out to meet him. He has refused one offer from him already and will not listen to a second.'

'I am well aware of that,' Liv replied. 'But I cannot allow you to ruin yourself so I can have a few illicit meetings.'

'I am not going to ruin myself,' she insisted.

'Not alone, perhaps. But you will have help,' her sister said in a grim tone.

'Mr Castell would never do such a thing,' she replied. Although there had been a moment when they were in her room that Peg had thought he quite wanted to.

Liv rolled her eyes. 'He entered this house under false pretences. You know nothing about his past or his parentage. It is possible he has not even given you his real name, since he's used two already.'

Peg struggled to find a counterargument, then she fell back on the only thing she had. 'Yet I know him, Liv. I understand him better than anyone I have ever met.'

Her sister reached out and cradled her face in her hands. 'That is only true because you do not know many people at all and even fewer men. This is what Hugh gets for keeping us both so sheltered. It has left you too naive to navigate the *ton*.'

'Do not treat me like a fool,' she said, pulling away from the comforting grasp. 'I know...what I know.' For a moment, she had wanted to say something about the contents of her heart, but it would have been premature and proved her to be just as naive as her sister thought her.

'And I know what I know,' Liv replied. 'Once he has got what he wants from you, he will go and not look back. If you are not careful, you will be unfit for a decent marriage in the future. And if you are unlucky, he will find enough information to bring the house down around us. I hope you will be satisfied, then, with what you have learned.' Liv turned and left her, slamming the door of the sitting room as she went.

After a good night's sleep, David felt no better about his conversation with Peg. He had not wanted to, but he had dreamed about her, smiling at him and rushing into his arms. She had answered his kisses with her own and whispered her hopes to him as if they had any possibility of a future together.

Even worse, the thought of her partnering him in his investigation excited him in a way that defied all logic. She had been a great help to him so far and could be so in the future, if he could think of a way to smuggle her out of the house to accompany him on his interviews.

But each new fact increased the chances that they would find a truth she was not expecting. She was fond of him now, but what would happen on the day they discovered that her brother had done the things he was accused of? He did not imagine her affection for him would last through that.

If the end result was going to be disaster, it was foolish to foster hopes in either of them. It was even more dangerous to kiss her and raise passions that dare not come to fruition. And yet…

When he arrived at Scofield House for the next faux dance lesson, his heart galloped at the knowledge that he would see her. The fact that they would be alone together for a precious hour raised an irrational joy that he could not smother. If love had come to him, it had found the worst possible time to do so. Even so, he could not bring himself to regret it.

When he arrived in the music room, Lady Olivia was waiting for him, but there was no sign of Peg. Though he had wanted an opportunity to question the other sister about the murders, there was something about the cold look she was giving him that made him doubt she was likely to share anything of import with him, now or ever.

But Peg was another matter. She would tell him anything he asked, even when he was not sure he wanted to hear it. He needed to remove the obstacle to their privacy before she arrived. He grinned at Lady Olivia in what he hoped was an encouraging way and went to the window to open it and help her out.

'Not so fast, *signor*,' she said in a voice that dripped irony.

'You do not want to visit with your friend?' he said.

'Not at the expense of my sister's honour,' she said, giving him a stern look. 'And you can drop the false accent, Mr Castell. Peg has already told me that you are no more an Italian than I am.'

'I am sorry to have deceived you over the matter of my birth. But I assure you, your sister is perfectly safe with me,' he said, holding his hands wide and empty before him.

'Pardon me if I do not take your word over the evidence of my own eyes,' she said.

'What is it you think you see?' he asked, trying not to look guilty.

'Nothing, when I look at you,' she said, putting a subtle emphasis on the first word to remind him where he ranked in her acquaintance. 'But that hardly matters since I know you are a liar and do not trust you at all. It is what I see when I am with my sister that worries me.'

'And what is that?' he said, trying not to seem too eager to hear the answer.

'I told her to flirt with you,' the lady admitted, with a regretful shake of her head. 'But it is clear she does not know how to keep a dalliance from becoming too serious. She is enjoying these lessons far too much. She cannot stop speaking of you. She glows,' Olivia said in disgust.

'She does?' he asked, feeling a matching flush on his own cheeks. This was far better than dallying with him because he was a lower-class novelty.

'And according to her maid, she lured you to her bedroom and trapped you in a kiss,' Lady Olivia said, somewhere between shocked and amazed. 'You may not be a gentleman, but you are a fully grown man and should have known better than to follow an innocent girl to her bedchamber.'

'She was very persuasive,' he replied, remembering the awkward kiss she had given him and trying to hide his smile.

'If you are wise, you will resist any further persuasions and do nothing to encourage her,' she said, shaking her head in disgust. 'My brother would not approve, and he has a certain reputation for violence that is well deserved.'

'Really?' he said, wondering if this was an idle threat or if she was about to reveal some unheard truth.

'Let us say, I have seen for myself what happens to men who pay court to me who do not meet his approval,' she said.

'Your friend who you visit with during the lessons,' he completed for her.

She shook her head. 'He is far too smart to run afoul of Hugh. I am thinking of another, more foolish young man, who ended up dead in a river.'

She had to be speaking of Sterling. He blinked in surprise for he'd heard nothing from his friend about a penchant for Lady Olivia. 'Surely you do not think the Duke is capable of murder.'

'I do not know what to think,' she said, her face clouding with confusion. 'I only know what I have seen for myself. And I would advise you, for Peg's sake and your own well-being, to be more careful in your interactions with my sister.'

'I will take your words to heart,' he said, wondering if it would be possible for Peg to get more information out of her.

Suddenly the door opened and Peg entered, looking at the two of them with narrowed eyes. 'I had no idea that it was time for our lesson with Mr Castell. Someone seems to have set the clock in the morning room back a quarter of an hour.'

'How strange,' replied her sister, giving her a blank look.

Peg stared back at her. 'It is good to see that one of us knew the correct time.'

Lady Olivia tapped the watch pinned to her bodice and smiled.

Peg walked to the window and opened it with a yank that sent the sash crashing upward. 'I would not want you to be late for your appointment with Alister,' she said, offering an artificial smile.

'He will not mind if I am needed elsewhere,' Olivia said, eyes locked on her sister.

'You are not needed, or wanted,' Peg snapped. 'Now go on your own before I push you out that window.'

Lady Olivia held up her hands in surrender and walked to the window. As she straddled the sill she gave David a final look of warning before disappearing from sight.

Peg slammed the window shut after her, then turned to him, obviously still furious. 'What did she say to you?' she demanded.

He smiled back at her, hoping to dissipate her anger. 'I am not sure, but I think she just told me that your brother killed Dick Sterling because he offered for her.'

It seemed he had succeeded for her eyes went wide and her jaw dropped in amazement.

'She also said I should stay away from you, because you are getting too attached to me,' he added, then waited to see how she responded.

'Liv needs to mind her own business,' she replied with a wave of her hand. 'She has problems of her own if she thinks Hugh is murdering her suitors. She had best worry about Alister and leave me to make my own decisions.'

She had not admitted that she had feelings for him, but neither did she deny it. It gave him reason to hope. He gave her his most winning smile. 'And what sort of decisions might those be?'

She folded her arms in front of her and gave him a considering look. 'She said I must not get attached to a man I know nothing about.'

'This is probably true,' he agreed, feeling his chance slipping away.

'So, you must tell me more about yourself. You know almost everything about me and are learning more about my family with each day that passes. But I know very little about you. When you are away from me what sort of life do you lead, precisely?' she asked.

He shrugged, wishing he could deflect this sudden curiosity that would only call attention to how different they were. 'There is nothing that would interest you, I'm sure.'

'But I am interested,' she insisted. 'How does one decide to become a newspaper reporter?'

'Not everyone is born to the gentry,' he reminded her with a sad smile. 'Some of us have to work for a living. But if you must know, I decided on it when I was in school.'

'You went to school,' she said, eyes wide. Then she covered her mouth in embarrassment, probably fearing that she had insulted him again.

'A very good school,' he assured her. 'I am a natural son, but my father, Lord Penderghast, acknowledged me from the first. He saw to it that I was properly educated.'

had continued to claim innocence, even as he was walked to the gallows.

'And was he innocent?' she asked, leaning forward.

'I seriously doubt it. He was found after the last killing holding a knife and covered with blood,' David replied. 'But I suspect there is not a man alive who will not claim innocence to save their own neck from the noose.'

'And some of them are telling the truth,' Peg said, with a firm nod. 'You have seen the worst of mankind, so of course you find it hard to believe, but not all those accused are guilty.'

'And you mean to prove it to me,' he said. The smile she was giving him was so brilliant that he almost wished she could succeed.

'Once all the evidence has been gathered, you will see that you have been mistaken about Hugh,' she replied. 'But I cannot think of anything here that will prove it to you.'

'I have been giving thought to how best we might proceed in our investigation,' he replied, wondering if she would be brave enough to do what he was going to suggest.

At this, she brightened and leaned forward, eager to hear what would come next.

'I am afraid Mr Castellano is about to come down with an ague that will make lessons impossible for some days,' he said, holding up a hand to stop her protest. 'You and your sister will decide to go shopping instead.'

'And do you see him often?' she said, probably imagining that he was a beloved member of the family.

'No,' he replied with a tight smile. 'We have seldom spoken. I think his generosity is in some way attached to the hope that he need never communicate with me, outside of a signature on the occasional cheque.'

'I see,' she replied, her face clouding with what looked like pity.

'It does not matter to me,' he said hurriedly. 'I have got all I need out of him. Once I had matriculated, he gifted me with a settlement sufficient to set me up in the business of my choosing.'

'But you are not close as a father and son should be,' she reminded him.

'You mean, like your father and brother,' he reminded her.

'Despite what you think, they were very alike,' she said.

'Yet it does not appear to have ended well,' he replied.

She shook off his suggestions, turning the conversation back to him. 'So, your estranged father gave you a settlement. What did you do with it?'

'I scrimped while I was in school, using as little of my allowance as I could and avoiding foolish pastimes that most of the boys took part in. I combined what money I had saved with his final gift and invested it, living off the earnings of what jobs I could find until such time as the returns on the investment came in,' he said. 'While I was in school,

I enjoyed writing and have always had a healthy curiosity. So, I presented myself to a local newspaper and proclaimed myself willing to write whatever it was that was needed for whatever they were willing to pay me.'

'And you made a success of it?'

'Not at first,' he admitted. 'It was dashed hard to get assignments and even harder to get paid for them. But I persisted and have made a comfortable living at it, while continuing to tend the nest egg.'

'How interesting.' Now her eyes were wide with approval at his apparent ingenuity.

He laughed. 'Only a person raised to have no occupation can be that fascinated by regular employment. All the same, I thank you.'

She blushed. 'You must think me terribly silly. Sometimes I cannot seem to find the right words to speak to you.'

'That is because we are very different,' he reminded her. 'You have been sheltered from people like me. You can hardly be blamed for it, since any man of sense wants his sisters to live lives free of care. I am doing well now, but a few years ago I missed more meals than I ate and lived in a room smaller than the one you would give to a maid.' And there was the truth of it. Now she must see that he was nothing.

'You worked hard until you could live comfortably,' she said.

He nodded, surprised at the pride he heard in her voice, as if she shared in the joy of his success.

Now she frowned. 'I have never known a life other than the one I have right now. But, sometimes, I think it had been a little too safe,' she said. 'It cannot be good for the character to be so completely isolated from the rest of the world that one does not see what is going on under one's very nose.'

It was probably true. When he had come to this house he had expected Peg and her sister to be as vapid and foolish as many of the ladies of the *ton*. It had been a relief to find that he was wrong. 'Your curiosity about others does you credit,' he assured her. 'It is one of your many appealing qualities. It is no fault of yours that you have had little opportunity to exercise it.'

'It is not that I object to the way my brother treats me,' she said hurriedly. 'As you say, he has my best interests at heart.'

'But you long for adventure,' he said with a nod.

'And you have had them,' she said. 'Tell me about the things you have written.' She pulled up one of the little gold chairs in the corner of the room and gestured to a second one for him.

He sat down, stretching his legs. 'Well, now. Let me see. There must be some stories fit for a lady's ears.' He began to recount a tale of a series of robberies from great houses in Sussex and the discovery that a local vicar was pilfering things as he made visits to his parishioners. He followed this with the case of a notorious murder in the West End and the interview he had done with the man who was charged. He

'But my brother's men will never allow a meeting,' she reminded him. 'I am quite sure we are followed wherever we go to prevent us from getting up to the sort of things you are planning.'

He reached into his pocket and pulled out the list of directions he had created for her. 'I will take care of the men who are following you. You and your sister must follow this route to the letter. If Lady Olivia wishes to meet with her Alister, he will find her at this address.' He tapped a line at the bottom of the page. 'I will come for you there, as well.'

'And then?' she asked, fascinated.

'I have not yet decided,' he lied. The destination he had in mind was the last place she belonged, but it was the next best place to search.

'It will be a surprise,' she said, as if they were going on a great adventure and not trying to find the information that could destroy her family. She glanced at the clock on the mantle. 'But that brings us to the question of what we should do with the half hour left to us today.'

He knew what he wished to do with the time and it was an even worse idea than the trip he was planning for her. He cleared his throat. 'What do you wish to do?'

'I do not want to waste it dancing,' she said, leaning forward in her chair so he could hold her.

For a man who was supposed to ruin her reputation, David Castell was surprisingly missish. Her approach seemed to startle him, which made her worry that her advances had become unwelcome. Had Liv really threatened him to the point where he did not want her?

Then he leaned forward and reached for her, as well. Once his arms were around her, he whispered, 'I should not allow myself to be persuaded so easily. But I have wanted this from the first moment I saw you.'

'Really?' she said.

To prove it, his head dipped forward and their lips met. It was the best possible answer, far better than words. He showered her mouth with a series of brief kisses before setting there, easing her lips apart.

She relaxed and let him take her mouth with slow strokes of his tongue. Eventually he eased away and settled his mouth against her ear to whisper, 'I dream about making love to you.'

'You do?' She wished she could say the same, but she had been afraid to even think about it, much less dream that it might happen.

His hand crept up her body to settle over the swell of her breast, giving it a gentle squeeze. 'I think of what I will do if we could find a place to be alone, even for an hour.'

'Tell me,' she whispered back.

'I would have you out of this dress and I would kiss every inch of your body,' he said, nipping the lobe of her ear.

The words sent a shudder through her that seemed to start somewhere deep inside. 'Tell me more,' she said, wanting to feel that excitement again.

'Do you understand what happens between a man and a woman, when they are in love?' he asked.

She had a vague idea, but she shook her head, wanting him to explain it to her.

He chuckled and each puff of air chased up and down the nerves of her body like sparks. Then he began to talk. He described the most intimate part of her body to her, explaining the delicious sensations he could raise in it.

In response, she felt the words on her skin, as gentle as the touches he described. The sensation hummed through her body and she felt herself opening to him, like the flowers he compared her to.

He described his own body to her, his words hard and rough and full of need. And as she leaned into him, she could feel his hard-muscled thigh pressing against her leg. He told her of their joining and something seemed to burst and flood through her, leaving her shaking in his arms.

He laughed again, soft and approving. 'My darling. My sweet love. My dreams will not live up to the reality of you.'

She was not sure what he meant, but she felt much the same thing about him. If the way she felt now was a foretaste of what could happen in the future, then love must be very wonderful indeed.

Her sister's whistle came from the garden and he leaned back in his chair, taking a steadying breath before reaching out to tuck a loose lock of hair behind her ear. 'Go to her,' he whispered. 'And remember. Tomorrow, we meet on Bond Street.'

She nodded and went to the window, trying to pretend that her life had not just been changed by a whisper and a kiss.

Chapter Ten

As he had promised, the next morning they received a letter announcing that Mr Castellano had taken ill and would not be giving lessons until the worst had passed.

Olivia was put out by the news since it meant a change in her plans, as well. It took some time for Peg to explain the urgent need to use the time shopping on Bond Street and the fact that it would be possible to meet with Alister for as long as she liked, if he arrived at the address she provided.

'And what will you be doing, while I am with him?' Liv said, folding her arms in a show of resistance.

'You have not been troubled to leave me alone thus far,' Peg reminded her. 'Now is not the time to start. Besides, I will be safer wandering through the shops than I am at home.'

'That is probably true,' Liv agreed, relaxing somewhat, though still obviously suspicious. 'But I do not understand what you are up to that requires leaving the house at all.'

'The less you know about that, the better,' Peg said. 'If Hugh gets wind of it, he will be most unhappy and you will not want to be complicit.'

Liv waved her hands in surrender. 'You are right. Whatever is happening, I do not want to know of it. But it is a comfort to know that, if we are discovered, you will be in far more trouble than I am.'

They waited until afternoon, so that the trip could be attributed to normal boredom and not a substitution for the missing lesson. Then they set out together through the front door on their feigned shopping excursion.

Behave normally. That was what David had said. But now that Peg was called on to do it, it was much harder than it appeared to act as if nothing was unusual. As they walked out towards Bond Street, she knew that they were being followed by agents of her brother, just as they always were when they left the house. But today, the back of her neck itched with the feeling of eyes marking her every move.

She took a deep breath and focused on the pavement in front of them, clutching Olivia's hand.

'This is a disaster in the making,' her sister muttered through barely parted lips. 'Hugh will know of our movements by supper and we will never be allowed out again.'

'We will be fine,' Peg replied with the faintest of nods. 'David has a plan.'

'So it's David now, is it?'

She dipped her head so the brim of her bonnet could hide her blush. 'It seems silly to call him by his last name, now that I know him better.'

'Remember what I told you about flirtations with the dancing master,' her sister said, trying to sound stern.

'It is not a flirtation,' she responded. In truth, it had become much more than that. 'I just want to prove to him that he is wrong about Hugh.' Because, if he was right, there was no hope for anything more between them.

Liv responded with a sceptical stare. 'Very well. If you think you can find our brother innocent, then I am eager to see you try. But I do not want to see you disappointed…' she paused '…in Hugh, or with your friend David.'

Peg responded with what she hoped was a knowing laugh. 'You do not have to worry about me. My heart is not so easily engaged as that.'

'Of course not, wise woman of the world,' her sister said with a doubting smile. 'But today, you must show me why you have such faith in the man.'

'We will see soon enough if he is worthy of it,' Peg replied and gave a subtle inclination of her head. 'According to his note, we are to turn quickly at the next corner.'

They did as instructed and disappeared down the side street and then turned down an alley before their followers could catch up with them. Peg counted out doorways, pulling her sister into an inauspicious

entryway and shutting the door behind them. They
found themselves in a dimly lit hallway and walked
to its end, turned right and followed the next passage.

When Peg was almost ready to give up hope that
they would ever see the outside world again, they
emerged in the storeroom of a haberdashery, streets
from where they had begun. When they stepped into
the main room of the shop, Alister was waiting for
them, just as he had been instructed.

He gave Peg a pleased nod before holding his
hands out to Liv. 'Darling.'

'Alister,' she replied with a surprised smile, as
if she had not believed that their plan would work.

He looked back to Peg. 'You are all right returning to your home unescorted.' The lack of question
in his tone implied that the answer had best be yes,
since he was not interested in being her escort or
having her accompany them.

'I will be fine,' she said, smiling as if she had
not noticed the dismissal. Hopefully, she was telling the truth. As yet, she had seen no sign of David.
She would feel a total fool if he had led her on some
goose chase, stranding her on a side street without a
maid to guide her home.

Her answer seemed to satisfy Alister, for he turned
back to her sister without waiting for further confirmation. 'Let us be off.' Without another thought for
her, they disappeared out the front door of the shop
and set off down the street, hands clasped and heads
dipped in intimate conversation.

Peg felt a moment of envy, followed by a profound feeling of loneliness. She still had the memory of David's kisses, his passionate words, and the way he looked at her when no one else was around. But it would be foolish in the extreme to fall in love with someone who was an enemy to her family. It was even worse that he seemed to be just as attracted to her. There should be at least one sane head in the relationship to call a halt to what they were doing before they did something they'd be sorry for.

But for now, her only regret was that she was alone in the shop. Where was he?

When she was almost ready to give up and find her own way home, a hired carriage pulled up on the street outside. The door opened and David hopped to the ground. When he spied her through the window, his face lit with a smile and he gestured to her to come out and join him.

'You got us transport,' she said, wondering where they were going.

'It seemed like the sensible thing to do. Your brother's men were following close behind you when I distracted them and I did not want to risk their guessing our direction and rounding the corner to catch you before we could make away.'

'You handled that well,' she said with a smile.

He gave a brief bow of thanks as he helped her up into the carriage. Then he gave an address to the driver and they set out.

'So, you had a destination in mind,' she said, watching the streets pass by outside.

'Indeed. And it is a place no lady should go,' he said with a leer.

'A special treat, then,' she said, hiding her smile with a glove.

He shrugged. 'Not so very shocking, really. But I am sure that your brother would be appalled to find you have learned of the place.' They had turned off into a quiet residential square. They stopped in front of a small town house. She could see nothing about it that should be too very shocking so she looked to David for explanation.

He grinned. 'We are going to visit the *pied-à-terre* that your brother keeps for his mistresses.'

Her eyes went wide. 'My brother has mistresses?'

'Not currently,' David allowed. 'But we will be meeting with one of his previous ladybirds, who should be full of information.'

She could understand why he had said no lady should be here. She had already learned things that Hugh would not want her to know. But seeing an actual member of the demi-monde would be as exciting as going to the Tower of London to see the lions and bears. If she had wanted an adventure, this surely was one.

David reached into his pocket and produced a key, turning it in the lock and opening the door, looking both ways to be sure they were not observed before ushering her into the foyer and closing it behind them.

'How did you get that?' she said, pointing to the key in his hand.

'From the lady in question. She had a copy made while living here and neglected to return it to your brother.'

'And she gave it to you instead,' Peg said, with a raise of her eyebrow.

He replied with a shrug. 'I might have given her a small financial incentive.'

'You bribed her?' she said, surprised.

'Money is the best way to communicate with courtesans,' he said with a smile. 'Or so I am told.' He led her further into the house, to the sitting room, keeping the curtains drawn against intrusive gazes of neighbours and lighting candles to disburse the gloom. Then they waited.

A short time later, they heard the unlocked front door open and a woman walked into the room.

She was not at all what Peg had expected. She was strikingly pretty, with dark red hair pulled smooth away from her pale face. But she was dressed in a fashionable and modest walking ensemble, decorated with a single cameo brooch and not the flamboyant satins and jewels Peg had expected. Everything about this woman was subdued and ladylike. If she had been Hugh's mistress, Peg had to admire his taste.

'Miss Devereaux,' David said, rising to greet her. 'It is so kind of you to take the time to speak with us today.'

The woman took a moment before responding, looking around the room with fond remembrance. Finally, her eyes fell on Peg and she started in surprise. She looked away again, as if acknowledging the invisible distance between their ranks, before turning back to David. 'It was no trouble, Mr Castell. Although it was most bold of you to choose this particular meeting place.'

'I thought I would choose a space I knew to be both discreet and unoccupied,' he said.

Miss Devereaux went to a chair by the fire and sat, steepling her fingers and staring back at them. 'I assume you want to know the details of my relationship with the Duke of Scofield.'

David settled in his chair again and nodded. 'Your parting from him, most specifically. But anything you wish to tell us will be most illuminating.'

She glanced at Peg again. 'He will be most unhappy with me if he finds out I have spoken to you. But he will be absolutely livid should he find that Lady Margaret was present for the conversation.'

'He will never find out from me,' Peg said hurriedly.

'Do you fear his response?' David said, ignoring the social embarrassment.

'Physically?' The woman paused, as if considering. 'No. He never gave me reason to worry on that account. But he is a very powerful man and we did not part under the best circumstances.'

'And why, precisely, did you part?' David asked.

'I found another protector that I preferred,' she said, with a faint blush.

'And what was the name of that man?' he prodded, gently.

'Richard Sterling,' she said.

'And what happened after you told the Duke that your affections had waned?'

'He requested that I leave his house,' she said, giving another fond look at what had been her sitting room.

'And did you move into rooms provided by Sterling?' he asked.

She nodded. 'He was most generous.'

'And are you still with him?' David asked.

'You know I am not,' she snapped, fishing in her reticule for a handkerchief to wipe away a tear. Once she had composed herself, she said, 'Shortly after we came to our arrangement, he died.'

'He was murdered,' David corrected.

'Must you make me go through the details that you already know?' she said, her voice unsteady.

Peg reached out a hand and laid it on David's in warning, then looked to the other woman. 'We understand this is painful for you and we are sorry to be upsetting you.'

'Thank you,' Miss Devereaux said softly, giving her a damp smile and wiping her eyes again.

'You know things that we do not,' David reminded her. 'Do you remember what you discussed the last time you saw him? Did he mention the Duke?'

She nodded. 'The last night we were together, Richard had just come from his club where he'd seen Hugh, who was exceptionally drunk. Threats were made.'

'Exactly what kind of threats?' David pushed.

'Hugh threatened to kill him,' she said with a sigh.

David turned to Peg with a triumphant smile, as if it was a surprise that her brother, when drunk or angry, would make wild statements. Instead, she turned to the courtesan and asked the question she wanted answered. 'Why did you leave my brother?'

'I preferred Richard Sterling,' she said, with a gentle smile.

'But why?' Peg demanded. 'I am sorry if I am speaking of something I should not, but I had always assumed that women of your profession preferred men of wealth and power. Surely a rich duke would be more reliable than a common gentleman.'

'True,' Miss Devereaux replied. 'But there is a matter of personal pride, as well. If I am honest, Scofield was never particularly interested in me.'

'Was he blind?' David asked in surprise.

This made the other woman laugh. 'To some things, perhaps he was. He gave me many gifts and made a generous settlement on me, even after I told him I was leaving. But it surprised me that he would argue with Richard over me, since, when I was his to command, his heart and mind always seemed to be engaged elsewhere.' She smiled. 'It was most refreshing to be with Richard, who was quite devoted to me.'

Peg cast a glance in David's direction and saw a flash of surprise, followed by a look of deep cogitation.

When no further questions came from either of them, Miss Devereaux stood to go. 'I hope that was sufficient, because I cannot think of another thing that I might share with you.'

David stood, offering her a bow. 'You have answered anything I could think to ask. Thank you for your help.' Then he escorted her to the door.

When he returned a short time later, Peg was ready for him. 'I hope this has convinced you that my brother could not have killed your friend over that woman. We have already established that he was in love with someone else.'

'Have we?' he said, doubtful.

'To my satisfaction, yes, we have,' she said. 'But Miss Devereaux is something else entirely. She admitted that he did not care enough to keep her. I doubt his apathy for her would extend to fatal violence towards the man who took her away.'

'Perhaps not,' David agreed, yielding far too easily. 'But he had other reasons to argue with Sterling.'

'I suppose you mean the fact that he denied Mr Sterling the opportunity to court Olivia,' she said.

He nodded. 'And Dick responded by taking his mistress away from him.'

The idea that a supposed gentleman could behave in such a way made her stomach churn. 'Then Hugh was right to deny him access to Liv. He does not sound like a very nice person.'

'He was my best friend,' David reminded her.

'Then I do not think too highly of your choice in companions,' she said.

'With your brother's history, you cannot point fingers,' he reminded her.

'My brother's alleged history,' she replied, annoyed. 'Whereas, your friend's behaviour towards my sister is, at best, fickle, and, at worst, devious.'

'He still did not deserve to be murdered,' David countered.

'And you still cannot prove that my brother had anything to do with his death,' she finished. 'He might have been set upon by footpads. Or perhaps he treated someone else as despicably as he did Liv.'

'It was not your sister that he meant to spite,' David said in a logical tone. 'It was your brother. He could not have your sister, so he took Scofield's woman away from him.'

She could not control her inarticulate cry of rage. 'You speak of living, breathing women as if they are pawns on a chessboard to be moved and captured and easily replaced.'

David opened his mouth, then closed it again, as words failed. Then trying again, he began in a conciliatory tone, 'Now, Peg...'

'That is what you have to offer?' She laughed. 'It sounds as if my understanding of the situation is accurate and you are about to explain to me that it is not as bad as it sounds.'

'Well...' he added and made a vaguely calming gesture with his hands that only made her angrier.

'I should have known that a man who came to my house under a false name to manipulate me into giving him information would be surrounded by similar men who are equally horrible.'

'I am horrible now, am I?' he said in surprise.

'You did not seem to think so yesterday, when I was kissing you.'

'I was a fool,' she said, appalled that her desire had been so easily aroused. 'My brother is right to protect me from socialising with men, because it is clear that kisses and soft words are all it takes to turn me against my family.'

'Stop pretending that you have no will of your own,' he snapped. 'You have been in control of this situation from the first and have changed the direction of my plans far more often than I have manipulated yours. I did not have to seduce you into helping me. You volunteered.'

'And now I am leaving.' She stood, wiping her hands down her skirts as if it were possible to get rid of the sordid nature of the things she had learned.

'I am sorry if you do not like the things you have heard today,' he said in a softer tone. 'But you were the one who insisted on coming along. If you cannot steel yourself against unfortunate truths, then perhaps it is best we part. I guarantee you, there will be more of them before this is over.'

He was talking of Hugh again, still convinced of his guilt. It exhausted her to think about that. Life would be so much easier if she had never met David Castell. She shook her head, resisting the urge to cover her ears. 'Send for the coach, please. I wish to go home.'

'But, Peg…' He sprang to his feet, as if ready to stop her, but on seeing her angry expression, took a step away. 'I will signal the driver.' He went to the door, leaning out to wave down the street to bring the equipage forward.

She went to his side without waiting to be retrieved, adjusting her bonnet and tugging at her gloves, so she would not have to look at him as they waited.

'I do not want things between us to end this way,' he said softly.

'That is not for you to decide,' she replied, staring past him at the closed door.

'Whether we are together or apart, the question of your brother's guilt or innocence remains.'

He was right. If she left him alone, he would report what he wanted and reject what he did not. Her brother needed her to support him, if no one else would. 'I do not wish to discuss it now,' she said. She was still far too angry to speak with him.

'Here are the directions for tomorrow's meeting,' he said, pressing a folded sheet of paper into her hand. 'You can decide before then if you are interested in seeing this through to the end. No matter what, know that I will be waiting for you.'

Chapter Eleven

To say he had handled the day badly was an understatement.

When he had planned for the interview in Scofield's apartment, he'd had some hopes that the secluded location might give them time to explore something other than the mystery they were trying to solve. They would be totally alone with no chance of interruption and he had hoped to make good use of the time.

Instead, he had allowed her to think that he viewed women as a commodity to be swapped and traded between men, with no thought to their feelings. But it had not been his fault at all. He was not the one keeping a mistress, nor had he made advances on her sister only to turn his attentions to Miss Devereaux to spite the Duke.

It had been done by his best friend. And when the time came to deny that friendship and admit Sterling had been a cad, he'd baulked. When he'd been alive, Dick's antics had been amusing. Neither of them had given a thought to whom he might have hurt by them, until the day he had gone too far and got himself killed.

The fact that it was now easier for David to see the motive for Dick's murder did not mean he was not deserving of justice. If behaving like a rogue with women was reason for an untimely death, half the men in London would be at risk. No, David was just as set as he ever was on proving that the Duke had killed his friend.

But it all became more complicated now that he'd found Peg. He did not want to lose her over today's stupidity, but she had to know that, with each clue they found, she was coming closer to the day she would have to choose between her loyalty to Scofield and her own future.

It was unrealistic of him to see himself as part of that future, but he could not seem to help himself. After her brother's downfall, everyone else might abandon her, but as he had told her when parting, even if she did not want him, he would still be waiting for her. Then, perhaps she would see his worth.

But the moment would never come if he could not persuade her to come back to him now. What could he do to help his case? When spoken words failed, he often did better with a written apology. But there was no way to get it to her, with the post watched by her brother and the servants. There was nothing to do but wait out the hours to see if she arrived at the appointed meeting place on the next day.

He got barely any sleep, anticipating the day to come, and rose in the middle of the night to write to her and unburden his feelings. Though it was possible that she might never see it, he had to hope that she would give him one more chance, if only to attempt to clear Scofield.

The next day, he went to Bond Street far earlier than was needed and wandered to the side-street shop where they were to meet. He should have kept to the original schedule for it gave him far too much time to think about the fact that she might not be coming at all. Perhaps he had already ruined his chances with her and would spend the day waiting in vain.

But shortly before the appointed time, Alister Clement appeared, loitering outside the shop as David was doing. It gave him hope, for he doubted that Peg would stay at home and send her sister out alone. A short time later, Clement snapped to attention and disappeared into the shop, returning with Lady Olivia on his arm.

David waited a few moments until they were out of sight before entering the shop himself to retrieve Peg. She was there, admiring a case of painted fans, hardly recognisable under the heavy veil he had suggested she wear.

He came up beside her and touched her lightly on the arm. 'Our coach awaits.'

She raised her head in recognition, but said nothing in response until they were shut up in the carriage and safely alone. Then, she raised her veil and turned to stare at him, her expression sombre. 'What are your plans for the day?'

He reached into his pocket and found the letter he had written her on the previous evening, thrusting it towards her. 'First, my apology for yesterday.'

Her eyes widened and as she read, her harsh expression eased into something warmer. When she was finished, she tapped the paper lightly against her knee. 'This is…'

'Insufficient. I know,' he said. 'There is so much more I could say.'

'No,' she said hurriedly, folding it and tucking it into her reticule. 'It is fine as it is.'

He smiled, relieved. 'That is good to know. I did not mean to offend you. And I am sorry that my friend was not more worthy of your sister's affections. But you must believe that I am not like that.'

'I think it will take more time for you to prove the fact to me,' she said with a slight smile. 'That is why I am giving you a second chance to do so.'

He relaxed back into his seat as the tension of the previous day released. 'Thank you.'

'Now, will you tell me our goal for the day?' she asked, adjusting her bonnet.

'We are going to interview a member of your brother's club,' he said. 'That is why you must be veiled. We cannot have him recognising you as Scofield's sister—for your sake and for the sake of the investigation.'

'Of course,' she agreed, dropping the lace back into place. They had arrived at the little house again, and he let them in using the key, escorting her to the sitting room and waiting for a knock at the door. He went to answer and returned to introduce her to the visitor.

'This is Mr Hathaway,' he said to Peg, offering the man no return introduction to her. 'He has agreed to help us fill in the details of the time before Dick Sterling disappeared.'

'For a price,' Hathaway reminded him. 'I would not normally consider it, but I am a little short on funds at the moment, and...' He turned out a coat pocket to demonstrate that it was empty.

'Of course,' David said smoothly, reaching into his own pocket and producing a pile of pound notes, resting them on his knee. 'But let us hear your story first. What happened on the night of April the fifteenth, this year?'

'I was at the club,' the other fellow said. 'Minding my own business, of course. But there are rare times when something happens that is impossible to ignore.'

'And what would that be?' David pressed.

'Scofield arrived after dinner. He was already the worse for drink and in a hell of a temper.'

Peg gasped beneath her veil, either at the curse or the unflattering description of her brother.

David considered warning the man to watch his language in the presence of a lady, but decided he did not deserve even that much information about Peg, lest he try to guess her identity. 'And was Scofield often in that condition?' David prompted, returning to the interview.

'That month?' Hathaway smiled and nodded. 'He was more moderate, before and since. But that was the month that his mistress left him. It was a great public embarrassment.'

'And he responded badly to it?' David asked.

'He snapped at anyone who spoke to him and downed brandy after brandy until the porter began to worry that he might drink himself to death.'

'And how did this influence his behaviour around Richard Sterling?' David asked.

'Sterling was the man who stole his mistress,' Hathaway said with a laugh. 'Apparently, she threw Scofield over with no warning at all. It was not as if the fellow was ungenerous. As I understand it, he could offer her twice what Sterling could. But she did not seem to care a whit for the jewels and money. She took a fancy to Sterling and that was all that mattered.'

'Did Sterling gloat over his success?'

'He did indeed,' the man replied with a grin. 'He told all that would listen that we could not blame the lady for choosing the better man. It was no fault of his if he happened to be that.'

David could feel the woman on the other end of the sofa vibrating with indignation at this slight, but she said nothing.

'And did they meet often at the club?' David asked.

'Hell, no,' Hathaway said with a wave of his hand. 'The rest of the members did their best to keep the two of them apart. Scofield has the devil of a temper and we were not sure what might happen should the two of them meet face to face.'

'Until April the fifteenth,' David finished.

'Too true,' Hathaway replied. 'Dick had been playing cards at the club all afternoon, and there had been no sign of the Duke. But then he arrived, drunk as a lord and ready for a fight.'

David felt another outraged twitch from the veiled woman at his side. It must be difficult for her to hear what others thought of her brother. But she had come here for the truth and now she must face it.

'And what was Sterling's response to this?' David asked.

'He did not take it the least bit seriously. The Duke challenged him and he replied that he was not going to answer a man in no condition to make such threats. He suggested that Scofield try again tomorrow when the wine was out of his system.'

'What did the Duke say to that?'

'It only made him angrier. He issued a series of insults, any one of which would be sufficient to instigate a duel. Sterling laughed at all of them, reminding him that he was not as foolish as to challenge a peer, much less be insulted by a man who was too drunk to know the repercussions of his words.'

'What did the Duke do then?' David asked, leaning forward in his seat, eager for the rest of the story.

'He cursed Sterling, his mother and all his family, and said if the man would not meet him on the field of honour, he would kill him where he stood.

Then he lunged for the fellow's throat and had to be dragged bodily from the room.'

'Was Sterling frightened by the threat?'

'He did not seem to be. He announced that love made men do strange things and it would be unfair to hold the peer responsible for something he was likely to regret in the morning. All the same, we persuaded Dick to leave for the night, so as not to antagonise Scofield any further.'

'And was this the last time you saw Sterling alive?' David pressed.

Hathaway gave a sombre nod. 'He was pulled from the river two days later.'

'And Scofield,' he prompted. 'What was his reaction to the death of the man he'd argued with?'

'I would say he had no reaction at all,' Hathaway replied with a confused frown. 'The announcement of the death was made at the club when he was present. And, of course, those of us who were there for the argument looked immediately to him to see what he would say. He announced that it was unfortunate. But there was nothing in his expression to hint at sincere grief or regret.'

'Did he look guilty?' Peg blurted, unable to remain silent any longer.

Hathaway started at the sound of her voice, then answered her question. 'No, I would not say so. He showed no real emotion of any kind. We might as well have been telling him of the death of a stranger.'

David cast a glance in Peg's direction to watch for any reaction that might be seen through her disguise. She was very still for a moment, then asked, 'Did he seem surprised?'

Hathaway was still as well, thinking. 'I cannot remember. I do not think he was anticipating the news, if that is what you mean. There was no agitation in him before the word was brought to us. It seemed to be just another day to him.'

Peg nodded in response, apparently satisfied by the answer.

Hathaway had clearly come to the end of the story and was eyeing the stack of notes that David held out to him. David passed him the money without a word.

'I would rather this not get back to Scofield,' Hathaway said, tucking the money in his pocket. 'It would be dashed awkward if he were to think I was telling tales.'

'Awkward for all of us,' David said, with a quirk of his lips. 'Do not worry, I have no intention of revealing my sources.'

'Very good,' the other man said and rose and left without another word.

There was a moment of silence between them, now that they were alone. Then Peg slowly raised her veil.

'Well?' David said and waited for her reaction.

'It does sound rather incriminating,' Peg admitted. 'But I cannot imagine that my brother would be so stupid.'

David started. 'What do you mean by that?'

'In my experience, which has lasted the length of my life, he is quite the cleverest member of the family,' she said. 'And I cannot imagine, even while drunk, that he would threaten a man in public and go through with the murder without making an effort to disguise his part in it. If he did, everyone would suspect him.'

'That is exactly what happened in this case,' David reminded her.

'But would it not make more sense to wait a few days at least, so that such suspicions would die?'

'There is such a thing as a crime of passion,' David said. 'Perhaps he was unable to control his actions.'

Again, she could not seem to believe the obvious. 'There are many things I might call my brother,' she said. 'Dictatorial, stuffy, unreasonable…' Her words trailed off as she realised that they were hardly a defence. 'But the one thing I would never believe was that he was easily overcome by passion. When he is at home, he is almost excessively reasonable.'

'There is always a first time,' David said. 'Or in this case, a first and second time.'

Peg sighed. 'It just seems so far outside his character.'

'It is not definitive proof,' David agreed. 'But it is suspicious.'

'Perhaps,' she said. 'But you will have to find someone who has witnessed the crimes or seen some evidence that can be linked directly to Hugh. You will never get me to turn against him based on what appears to be the truth,' she said and rose to go. Then she stopped, as if realising that there was no point in storming out in a huff if she needed his help to get home.

As she sank back into her seat, he reached out to lay a hand on hers to reassure her. 'I do not expect you to change your opinion until you are sure. But you might be able to change mine if you can find some detail in the first murder that I do not know. What happened on the night your father died?'

'My recollections?' She furrowed her brow. 'I remember much of what happened after, but there is very little from what happened before.'

'Think,' he urged. 'You or your sister might hold a key that we do not even know is missing.'

She pulled her hand away from his grasp and pressed her balled fists against her forehead as if it might be possible to force the memories out of her head. Then, she closed her eyes and took a deep breath, trying to concentrate.

'There was an argument at dinner,' she said at last.

'Really,' he said. 'What was it about?'

'There were so many arguments,' she said, still trying to focus. 'They were always about money. Hugh had run through his allowance again. Father said it was because he was a spendthrift. Hugh said it was because the amount was insufficient to maintain a normal life.'

'And what did your father say to that?'

'He was adamant that there would be no increase. Hugh must learn to live within his means.'

'And your brother's response?'

'Was to remind Father that, when he died, the

money would all belong to Hugh and he would do what he wished with it. Then he stormed away from the table.'

David stared back at her, not bothering to comment on how damning this sounded, for she must realise that herself.

'This was almost two years ago,' she said, as if that justified it. 'He is a much different person now.'

'I am more concerned with who he was then,' David said.

Peg grimaced. 'I wish there were something I could remember that cast things in a better light.'

No wonder she had not wanted to remember. Her version of events sounded as damning as anything he had found about Scofield's temper. 'And what happened after dinner?' he asked, hoping for her sake that she could find some scrap of information that supported her beliefs.

'I went to my room to read,' she said with a shrug. 'I wish I could tell you otherwise. I was upstairs and on the far side of the house when the crime occurred, deeply engrossed in a novel. At half past eleven, I heard a commotion downstairs.'

'What sort of a commotion?' he pressed.

'There was screaming,' she said. 'And a few moments later, the sound of running feet. And then shouting. I went downstairs to see what the matter was and the housekeeper met me in the hall and escorted me right back to my room. There was already a hot water bottle and brandy waiting for me. She told me that Father had been killed and that it was nothing that anyone wanted me to see or be involved in.'

'So, you truly saw nothing.'

'I was not allowed downstairs until the next morning. By then, the body was gone and the room had been cleaned.' She shuddered, as if imagining what she had not seen. 'It was strange. I expected to feel more grief than I did at Father's passing. But, if I am to be honest, the house was a much better place without him in it. If you asked Liv, she would probably agree with me. Our father had little time or understanding for either of us.'

David blinked in surprise. 'Did no one mourn for the old Duke?'

'Of the three of us, Hugh was by far the most upset.'

'Really?'

She nodded. 'I did not see him do anything as extreme as crying. But he did admit that he regretted the things he'd said at dinner. And since, he has been a changed man, much more moderate in word and action.'

'At home, perhaps,' he reminded her. 'Remember what you have just heard.'

She shook her head. 'You asked me what I knew from home. When he is there, he displays a far more moderate temperament than he did before Father died. He is unreasonably strict with us, but he does not make mad threats or even raise his voice.'

'Very well,' he replied. 'But his change of heart immediately after the murder might have been the actions of a guilty man, trying to hide his involvement in a crime.'

'Or the perfectly reasonable changes necessary when he became a peer and the head of the household,' Peg countered. 'Once Father was gone, it fell on him, overnight, to grow to be the man the family needed. He changed from being just my big brother to the person responsible for my care and future.'

Her explanation sounded reasonable, until he remembered the way Scofield had behaved towards his friend. Apparently, any maturity he'd gained on taking the title had been short-lived. But it would do him no good to harp on it, if he wanted the continued trust and affection of the woman sitting beside him.

He reached for her hand again, twining his fingers with hers. 'Your loyalty to him does you credit. But what if you are wrong? What will happen to you when he is called to answer for his crimes?'

'Alleged crimes,' she corrected.

He gave a resigned shrug. 'For now, at least. But consider, for a moment, that I might be right. If he is found guilty of murder, they will likely strip the title from him. And where does that leave you?'

She gave him a sad smile. 'If you truly care about me, we must hope that will not happen. Now tell me what our next move will be.'

He reached into his pocket to check his watch. 'I had hoped to do more today. These rooms need to be searched before Scofield realises we have found them. But we must get you home before you are missed.'

She nodded. 'These shopping trips do not allow much time for substantive investigation. But suppose I were to sneak out of the house at night? After the household retires, no one will think to look for me until morning.'

His breath caught in his throat at the thought of so much uninterrupted time alone with her. 'Do you really think you can get away?'

She smiled. 'We will have to see, won't we? If you have a carriage waiting for me tonight at ten, in the street behind our back garden, I will find a way to escape.'

He brought her hand to his lips, pressing a kiss into the palm. 'I will come for you myself. But for now, we must get you home. We have a busy night ahead of us.'

Chapter Twelve

Once she was safely at home, Peg pulled David's letter of apology from her reticule to read again.

Dearest Peg

Dearest was a lovely way to begin. Not quite as good as 'my dearest', but it would do.

Despite the way my friend behaved to your sister, I assure you I would never treat your affection in such a casual way.

She stared at the words, trying to decide if she was reading too much into them. The next line was easier to understand.

I hold you in the highest esteem and am devastated that I might have ruined the bond we have developed by my careless support of a man who was unworthy of my loyalty.

He held her in esteem and felt they had a bond. That was much clearer.

I am desolate that I cannot come to you now and explain myself in person, and overcome with fear that it might be too late to make amends for my behaviour.

She traced the words 'desolate' and 'overcome' with her fingertip, as if it were possible to soak up some of the emotion imbued in them. While she had not actually wanted the man to suffer, it was flattering to think that he had done so on her account.

I eagerly await our next meeting and am hoping that I may prove my undying loyalty to you.
Yours, David

He had undying loyalty and was hers. She doubted he had meant it to be so, but it was the closest thing she had ever got to a *billet doux*. No matter what happened between them, she would keep it always.

She had been angry with him after their last meeting. All that was sensible in her had argued that their association had been a mistake and would not end well. There was simply too much that she did not understand about the world outside Scofield House and the men that inhabited it. Perhaps he did not mean to use her, as Sterling had Miss Devereaux. But if she stood between him and his goals, she did not trust him to put her needs before his desire for revenge.

But though common sense had told her to forget him, when the time had come to plan her day, she had got out the directions he had given her and told Liv to prepare for another trip to Bond Street. She could not seem to resist seeing him again.

Perhaps she should blame Hugh and the strict rules he had set for her. Now that she had found a man willing to pay attention to her, it was difficult to let him go. Who knew when, or if, she would ever again have someone writing of his 'undying loyalty' to her? This might be her one and only chance to make memories that would have to last her through the cold isolation of spinsterhood.

That fear had inspired her to make the daring suggestion of meeting at night. They would be alone for far longer than they had ever been, in a place that had already been steeped in sin. If he acted on any of the things he had whispered to her the last time they had kissed, she did not think she would be able to stop him. Nor did she really want to stop him.

It was all very improper. Even her sister had warned her against risking anything more than kisses. It was proof that Liv knew less about love than she claimed. David's apology letter might make her think of for ever. But what if that could never be? If tonight was the only time they had together, she would not refuse anything he might suggest.

After dinner, she pretended to retire early, checking on her sister, who was already in her room with

Caesar planted on the end of her bed, worrying a pair of dancing slippers to shreds.

Then she went to her own room and summoned her maid, pinning her in place with a cold glare.

'My lady?' Jenny said nervously.

'I am going out,' she said. 'You do not know where and you had best keep this secret better than you did my last one, or I will dismiss you.'

'My lady,' she said, with a scared nod, then added, 'What do you wish to wear?'

For a moment, Peg considered dressing for seduction, then realised that even her best dinner gowns were quite modest, as befit a young lady who had not yet come out. Dressing up for this occasion would arouse nothing but the suspicions of her maid. Instead, she suggested her most plain and serviceable gown and a dark cloak that would hide her in the gloom as she made her way to the coach.

She looked at herself in the cheval glass and saw a woman who would not rate a second glance from even the most curious passer-by. She dismissed her maid and waited only a moment before creeping out into the hall, down the servants' stairs to the kitchen and out into the garden. From there, it was only a short run to the back gate and out into the street. At the end of the street, she could see the glow of two carriage lamps and the dark silhouette of a man, waiting on the walkway.

As she hurried in his direction, she saw him straighten to open the carriage door before catching her hand as she came beside him, swinging her up into a seat, joining her and closing the door, all in one smooth gesture. Before she had said a word, they were off.

'Lady Margaret, I presume?' David said from his shady corner of the cab.

She pulled back the hood of her cloak. 'It is fortunate that I am. You might have picked up a stranger off the street for all the time you took to check.'

She could see his smile in the gloom. 'Never. I would know you even in darkness.'

Perhaps it was the tone he used when he spoke the words, but there was something more than just confident familiarity there. It was as if he knew her because he had seen her a million times, in light and darkness and dreams. She remained quiet, her mouth dry from a sudden attack of nerves.

'I have brought extra candles and a lantern, if we should need one in our search,' he said, leaving her imagination behind and continuing in a most ordinary and practical way. 'They are probably not necessary—it is not as if we are exploring a cave—but it pays to be prepared.'

Was this an ordinary conversation? Or was he speaking a little too fast, as if trying to fill the empty air between them? Perhaps it was just the clandestine nature of their mission. Or perhaps it was because he was with her in a place where they both knew they should not be.

Now, he was looking at her, waiting for some response to anything he had said. 'You are unusually quiet this evening.'

She smiled and let out the breath she had been holding. 'I was trying to be so very quiet while leaving the house, I had forgotten it was safe to speak again.'

It did not matter if he believed this confusing explanation, he laughed at it and touched her hand. 'You are safe now. Safe as I can keep you, at least,' he added, lifting the back curtain of the carriage to make sure they had not been followed. 'It will be quite embarrassing if Scofield decides to use his rooms, now that we are on our way to them.'

'He was reading by the fire when I left him,' she said, relieved that she could put this worry to rest. 'When he is thus absorbed, he usually does not leave the chair until the book is done or the fire goes out.'

She could see a little of the tension go out of her partner. 'Excellent. It will be just us, then.'

'Just us,' she agreed.

They both fell silent for a moment, as if realising what that might mean.

Suddenly, the carriage jerked to a stop in front of their destination. Peg flipped the hood of her cloak back up to hide her face and let David help her out on to the street and quickly into the building, shutting the door behind them and rummaging in his pocket for the flint to light the candle he was holding. 'Make sure the curtains are closed in all the rooms,' he suggested as the light caught. 'We do not want to make the neighbours suspicious.'

She did as she was told, moving quickly from room to room to make sure that no ray of light es-

caped to the street. Then she turned to look around
the little apartment, lit in candlelight. It was a pleas-
ing arrangement of rooms, charmingly decorated. If
one did not know what it was used for, it was possible to covet the space and the privacy that one did
not get in the main Scofield town house, or the great
house in the country.

She could not help but find it cosy and much more
romantic than it had been in daylight. She could easily imagine her brother retreating here to visit one
woman or another. The thought made her blush,
but it also raised a hint of desire. This was a place
where anything could happen and no one would be
the wiser.

But as yet David had not asked anything of her.
Assumptions might lead to disappointment. And it
was probably unladylike to demand that he seduce
her immediately, when there was still work to be
done. 'Why have you not searched these rooms already?' she asked, running a hand along the back
of a sofa.

He hesitated. 'It belonged to Miss Devereaux during the time I was most interested in. And I have no
evidence that your brother used it at all during the
time your father was alive.'

'I doubt he'd have had the money to keep a separate residence then,' she agreed. 'Most of their arguments were about how parsimonious Father was
with allowances.' She went to the bookshelves, picking up a current novel and setting it back in its place.
'Even so, you have had the key to these rooms for

some time. Why did you decide to wait until I was able to help you do the searching?'

Was it her imagination, or had the question made him blush? It was hard to tell in the flickering light, but his ears seemed decidedly pink. 'You know your brother better than I do,' he said at last. 'The search will likely be more productive with your help.'

She had hoped he would admit that he wanted to be alone with her. Instead, his answer was the sensible one that she should have expected and she had to agree with it. 'If Hugh has retained the place when there is no resident, he must use it for his own purposes on occasion. I should think, if there are things he does not want his sisters to see, he would hide them here.'

'An interesting theory,' he said with a smile. 'And one that might not have occurred to me on my own.'

'Do not flatter me,' she said, taking down the books and paging through them, one by one. 'I need to be home before dawn and we have little time to waste.'

They went through the main room without finding anything of interest. The dining room was empty, as well. There was a small kitchen and a maid's room, both of which were devoid of any personal possessions that might be of interest.

Then they arrived at the bedroom. The wardrobe and dressers were empty, except for a very informative book of etchings in the table by the bed. She sat down on the edge of the bed and paged through it for a moment, before David came to her side and took it away, blushing.

'Surely you are not as innocent as I am,' she said, for there were things in the pictures that she had no idea were possible, much less done by decent people.

'I have more than enough experience to know what you are looking at,' he said, hiding a grin. He sat down beside her, holding the book just out of reach. 'It is meant to inspire passion.'

It was certainly inspiring something. Even after the brief glance she had got, her insides felt most peculiar. 'And do you often use such things?'

'Such things are not usually necessary when one is in the presence of a woman like you,' he said, placing the book back in her hands.

She opened it slowly, mesmerised by the image of a woman on her back, skirts hoisted to the waist, legs spread wide with her lover standing half-dressed between them. It was the most innocent of the drawings she had glanced at, yet it heated her blood in a most unexpected way.

When she looked up at David, it was to discover that he was not admiring the drawing, but staring at her, eyes hungry, his mouth set in an enigmatic smile. 'Does that interest you?'

'I…' She could not decide what to say. It fascinated her, as any forbidden fruit might. It represented everything that she was not supposed to know and not supposed to do, things she should not even ask about in the privacy of her rooms.

But now she was in a place even more private

than her own home, knowing they would not be interrupted for hours. She knew she should be frightened, or at least hesitant. Instead, she felt strange. Her clothes seemed to fit too tightly, her gown rubbing against swollen breasts, her legs heavy, wanting to spread like the girl in the picture, if only to allow some of the growing heat in her body to escape.

David stepped closer to her again, taking the book and setting it aside so it did not block the space between them. Then he bent down and kissed her on the mouth. She opened her lips for him, running her hands down the front of his waistcoat, trying to undo the buttons so she might touch the linen of his shirt.

He stopped the kiss for a moment, clasping her hands in his. 'Are you sure you know what you are asking for?'

'I have never been so certain in my life,' she said. It was a lie, of course. No amount of picture books could really explain what she suspected was to happen between them.

He shook his head and kissed her again, on the mouth and then the throat, tugging at the neckline of her gown until he found the buttons that held the front panel in place. He released them, one after the other, revealing the panel beneath that acted as her stays. He paused again, a finger hooked in the lacing. 'I hope you are sure, because we are about to do things that cannot be undone, should you realise you were wrong.'

He was trying to frighten her into retreat, but she did not want to stop. A chance like this, a man like this, might never come again. She wanted to enjoy each moment to the fullest. So she pushed his hand out of the way and unlaced the front of her gown, feeling her breasts slide down beneath the fabric of her shift.

He kissed her again, leaning forward until his fists pressed the mattress on either side of her hips. Then, his mouth dropped to her breasts, seeking out her nipples to suck them through the sheer cotton fabric that covered them.

Her back arched as he devoured her and her hands flailed, settling on the knot of his cravat, loosening it and pushing it out of the way so she could touch the skin of his throat, feeling it move as he kissed her.

He raised his head and put a hand to the back of her neck, urging her forward until her lips grazed the spot on his own neck where his pulse was beating. She pressed kisses there and into the hollows of his neck and shoulder, until he moaned and raised his hands to her breasts, massaging them in time to the sucking of her kisses. 'You are driving me mad,' he whispered, freeing one of his hands to grab hers and press them against the front panel of his breeches so she could feel the hard manhood beneath.

'Is that good?' she asked, confused.

'Very good,' he whispered back. 'It is the most delicious kind of torture. The only relief will come when I have made you mine. Not just for now, but for ever.'

'Show me,' she said.

He reached to the floor and bunched her skirts up

to her waist, allowing himself a single glance down and a deep sigh before looking into her eyes again. 'If you give me a lifetime, I will show you things that even that silly picture book cannot imagine. I want all of you, Peg, heart and soul and body.' With the tip of one finger on her chin, he brought her lips back to his for a brief kiss to seal his words.

'I am yours,' she said, arching her back, urging him to touch her.

In response, he pushed her back upon the bed and stepped between her knees as the man in the picture had done. His hands smoothed up the insides of her legs until he reached the place where her stockings ended so he could caress the flesh of her inner thighs.

She twitched, surprised at how sensitive the skin was, even more surprised as his fingers moved higher, settling at the delta where her legs met. At first, his touch relaxed her, making her legs fall open to give him better access. Then the pressure of his fingers increased, as did the pressure inside her body.

'You are mine,' he reminded her as his fingers grazed the opening of her body.

Muscles she'd never felt before were now on edge, flexing, preparing for use. She felt an urgent need for something she did not yet understand.

'You are mine and I am yours to do with as you please. I have been from the first moment I saw you, Peg Bethune. One look and I was lost.' He slipped a finger into her body and she was lost, as well. Her mind flashed to the pictures she had glimpsed in the bedside book and she reached for the buttons on his breeches, fumbling with them, eager to free him so they could find each other.

When she had released him, she was sure she had found the torture he had described before. He was hard in a way that must surely be painful, his member springing away from his body as if it longed for her touch. Hesitantly, she circled it with her palm, stroking once from root to tip.

His hand moved against her body, the fingers pressing deep into the soft wetness of it, moving in time to the beating of her heart. 'This may hurt you at first,' he whispered. 'Know that I love you and do not wish to cause you pain. I love you and, if you need me to, I will stop.' But there was agony in his voice, as if he made the admission against his will.

'Go on,' she urged, spreading her legs wider, lifting them as the girl in the picture had until her knees were bent and her feet rested on the mattress.

'Soon,' he groaned. 'Soon, my love.' The need inside her increased to uncontrollable desire as his fingers moved in and out of her body, his thumb brushing against a place of infinite sensitivity. She could hear herself begging, crooning his name as the pleasure took her last inhibitions away, her hand tightening on his member until he gasped.

Then he pulled his hand aside and stepped forward, pressing against her, letting her guide him past the point of pain and into her.

There was a moment of profound stillness when she knew her body was not totally her own. Then he clasped her hands in his, fingers twined, locking them together as tightly as their bodies were joined. He squeezed them, rubbing her palms lightly with his thumbs and making her shiver all over again. 'Even once we are gone from this place, remember this moment. We are together now, as I want us to be, my love. Now and for ever.'

He began to move. She focused on the feeling of his hands holding hers, firm but gentle, anchoring her to earth, as the pleasure came again, strong as a storm that was trying to wash her away from him. She would not lose him. Not now, not ever. She wrapped her legs around his hips and tightened her body around him, wanting to hold him there for ever, one with her.

The action seemed to drive him towards the same madness she felt and strokes became thrusts which became a trembling shuddering rush that raised an answering quaking in her. It rolled through them like thunder until she was sure that the house must be rocked from its foundations with the strength of their passion.

Then, the storm inside them broke, subsiding gradually into a mutual, exhausted suspiration.

His knees buckled and his head sagged forward as all the tension seemed to leave his body. He withdrew from her with a sigh, throwing himself down on the bed beside her so he could touch her face, his tongue tracing a lazy pattern at the base of her neck which gave her one final shudder of pleasure.

'Lady Margaret Bethune,' he whispered into her ear, 'have I told you how much I love you?'

'Do you really?' she said, snuggling against him.

'Do not sound so surprised,' he answered, nipping her throat in pleasant punishment. 'I adore you.'

'No one has ever said that to me before,' she said, still amazed.

'If you stay with me, you will hear it every hour of every day,' he said in a fervent tone, letting his lips rest on her skin. He reached into his pocket to check his watch, then began fastening his breeches. 'It is getting late. Or should I say, it is getting early. If we are to get you home before sunrise, we do not have time to dawdle.'

She sat up, alarmed, reaching for the watch so she might see.

He patted her hand. 'Do not worry. I will not let us be discovered. You are safe with me, always. But we had best get buttoned and laced and finish the last room.'

Safe. She did not feel that way. She felt dangerous and wild and reckless. Worse yet, she loved the feeling and did not want to lose it, even as his steady hands were returning everything to normal, helping her back into her gown, lacing the front and buttoning the panel, smoothing her skirts back down until they fell to her ankles.

He dropped a kiss on to the bare skin of her shoulder before doing up the last button. 'The next time we do this, I will make sure we have time to linger. I want to see all of you, next time.'

'The next time,' she said with a dazed smile. He

seemed so certain that there would be a next time. And the way this search was going, she was equally sure. There had been no conclusive evidence that her brother had done any of the things David accused him of. Soon, he would see that an exposé would be impossible. Once he had given up on the idea of punishing Hugh, they would be able to speak of the future. Then she would see if his talk of for ever was truth.

They went to the only room left, a small sitting room that appeared to share the duties of a library and office. David went through the writing desk, pulling out a stack of ladylike stationary and quills, as well as a larger pile of heavier paper, topped with the Scofield crest. 'It is clear he does some of his correspondence here,' David announced, holding up a quill. 'He has a very distinct shape when cutting his pen nibs. I recognise it from the study at the town house.'

'I wonder who he writes to that he would not want to include in the house post,' she said. 'It does not seem proper to come to one's mistress's house to write love letters to another woman.'

'It was not particularly proper for Sterling to be courting both your sister and Miss Devereaux,' he replied. 'Yet it happened.'

Peg shrugged. 'I have much to learn about men.'

'And I sincerely hope you never learn it,' he said, grinning and touching his hand to his forehead. 'You are far too quick a study already.'

She laughed. 'You did not seem to mind a few minutes ago.' Her laughter faded as she turned her attention to the books stacked on the shelves in a dark corner of the room. 'Oh, dear,' she said, looking at the titles.

'What have you found?'

She pulled out a book and handed it to him. *'Medical Enquiries and Observations, Upon the Diseases of the Mind.'*

'Interesting subject matter,' he said, opening the book and looking through it.

'And there are others,' she said, frowning. *'The Pathology of the Lunatic. The Anatomy of Melancholy. A History of Bethlehem Hospital. Care and Treatment of the Mad.'* She stared back at David, feeling real fear for the first time in their investigation. 'What was he trying to learn?'

David looked back at her, his eyes bright with discovery. 'Perhaps he was trying to find a cure for a personal problem.'

'No,' she said with a disbelieving laugh. 'No. That could not be right.' It was almost easier to believe Hugh a premeditated murderer than a madman.

'Can you think of what else it might be?' he prompted, giving her the chance to locate a defence. But, for the first time, she could not immediately come up with an answer. Then, a letter fluttered out from between the pages of the book that David was holding. He picked it up with a frown and read.

From the Head Keeper at the Hospital for Lunatics at Newcastle upon Tyne.

Salutations to His Grace, the Duke of Scofield.

We are honoured by your interest in our hospital and more than willing to answer the questions you have posited in your recent letter.

If the problem with your friend were of a simpler nature, we might be able to recommend a medicine that would minimise the uncontrollable mania and mitigate the episodes of rage. Large doses of laudanum might help, in conjunction with regular bleeding and cold water baths.

Unfortunately, when the problem has progressed to the level you describe and multiple deaths have occurred, it is too late for moderate treatment. If the law is not to be involved, then I recommend permanent residence in our hospital, where the patient can be restrained from harming themselves or others.

If you are interested, a tour of our facility can be arranged. It is also possible for us to come directly to London to collect the patient and take them under our care. If you require anything from us, you have but to write and I will be,
Your obedient servant,
Phineas Dial, Physician

The room seemed to be filled with a strange sound. Or perhaps it was her own hearing that was failing her and the roaring was in her ears. It was probably just the pounding of her heart, or the desperate struggle to take air into lungs that could not seem to function normally. It occurred to her that she might be about to faint, which was ridiculous for she had never been the sort of girl to fall into a swoon when shocked.

But then, she had never had a shock quite so large.

She barely felt David's hand as it took her by the elbow and led her to a bench by the window before she could fall.

'You understand what this means,' he said gently, then waited for her answer.

'No,' she insisted, not wanting to deal with the truth.

'You brother has been researching his personal demons, trying to find a way to control them,' David said, in a tone that could not be ignored.

'No,' she said again. But she could not seem to find the conviction to make herself believe the word.

'He has even gone as far as to consider permanent commitment,' David reminded her. 'No one writing about a "friend" ever truly has one.'

To this, she could not manage a single word of argument.

He continued. 'Even if you were to persuade me that there was a friend, Scofield clearly knows the identity of the murderer and has been complicit in hiding it from the public.'

She could not seem to control her breathing, which still came in short, shocked gasps as her mind raced over the events of the last few minutes. Had she been wrong, all this time? Was her brother really a madman who could not control his actions? Was she living with someone that might snap at any moment and take another life?

David had said he would help her get away before that happened. And after what they had done, she had assumed that, when this investigation was over, they would be together. But then, she had assumed that Hugh was innocent.

'Are you still going to publish?' she said, marshalling her panic and trying to see him as a reporter and not a lover.

'How could I not?' he said with a smile. 'This is the piece of information I was looking for. I am sure, after I speak to this Phineas Dial, I will have even more details. Perhaps even the letter that your brother sent, admitting that his supposed friend is a dangerous killer who might need to be incarcerated.'

'Then we are ruined,' Peg said, wrapping her arms around herself.

He sat down beside her, reaching for her hand. 'I warned you from the first that this was coming.'

She inched away from him with a shudder. She had been so sure that it would not happen, she'd ignored his warnings and befriended her destroyer.

Worse yet, she'd loved him. And now, if she went to him before or after the publication of his article, the world would see her as the fool who had betrayed her brother. 'He is sick,' she said at last. 'If he did what you think he did, he could not stop himself.'

'He is dangerous,' David corrected. 'You and your sister cannot stay with him. I will talk with Alister and we will get you both away from him.'

'But we cannot leave him,' she insisted, horrified. 'If he is ill, he will need us now, more than ever.'

He held out a hand to her. 'It would be better if you come away with me now, before things become difficult. The longer you stay, the harder it will be for you to leave,' he said. 'Once my article is published, all of London will know you as the sister of a murderer.'

'That is how they think of me now,' she said, rising and moving away from him. 'But I will not have them thinking that I aided in his downfall and then gave myself to his destroyer.'

She was surprised to see that he looked stricken. 'But I thought—'

'That there was a way to keep your original plan and have me, as well?' she interrupted. It had been almost as foolish as her plan, to turn him away from vengeance. Or the idea that she could lie with him once and not see the happy memory destroyed by reality.

'You said that my profession did not bother you,' he replied.

'Do not try to make this about your inferior birth,'

she snapped. 'I do not care that you have to work for a living. But that does not mean that I can look away as you use your glib writing against my family,' she replied. 'If you want me…if you love me, you will have to choose.'

'And if you loved me, you would not make me choose,' he replied. 'Scofield is a madman who murdered my best friend. He must pay for that.'

The room seemed to grow cold around her as she realised the magnitude of the mistake she had made. She had given her heart and her body to a man who would never want her as much as he wanted to see her brother hang. She moved as far away from him as she was able. 'It seems we are at an impasse. You must do as you must do and so must I. That means that what we have shared is over.'

'You cannot mean that,' he said with a disbelieving laugh. 'Only a few minutes ago, you swore you were mine for ever.'

'A few minutes ago, my world was very different than it is now,' she said, trying not to think of the letter and the promises she had made before seeing it.

'Your world is just the same,' he said softly. 'It is only your understanding of it that has changed.'

Perhaps he was right. When she was sure Hugh was innocent, she'd had hope. Now, it was gone, replaced by the bleak truth of what her future was likely to be. 'Then it is good that I know the truth. It will keep me from having any more foolish dreams about things…or people that I can never have,' she said, staring at him and reminding herself that she had promised herself memories, not regrets. 'Now, please, send for the coach that will take me home.' Because, despite all that she had done to help David Castell ruin it, home was where she belonged.

Chapter Thirteen

He wanted to argue. He wanted to scream at the unfairness of it and throw every word of love she had spoken back into her face until she acknowledged his pain. Instead, he did as she asked and summoned the carriage. He escorted her to the door and helped her up to her seat. When he went to climb in after, she stiffened and said, 'That will not be necessary. I can find my own way.'

'On the contrary,' he replied. 'Someone must pay the driver after.' In truth, there was no way he would allow a lady to travel unescorted so late at night. He needed to see her safely to the garden gate, at least. But he doubted she would be impressed by a show of chivalry now that she'd decided to cut out his heart.

Her lips pinched in an expression of distaste, but she made no further objections. They travelled in silence back to the neighbourhood of the Scofield town house.

* * *

The coachman stopped on the corner and David opened the door and let down the step, taking her hand to help her to the ground. He could still feel the gentle caresses that hand had given him in the bedroom, but now it was stiff as a marble statue inside her glove.

Then, she was walking away from him, down the street and disappearing through the gate without even a look back at him.

My God, what had he done? He had never laid himself bare before a woman as he had done for Peg Bethune. He had even told her that he loved her, though she'd given him no answering declaration. Instead, she had thrown his devotion back in his face and made him feel like a lovesick fool.

Yet he could not stop thinking about her. Perhaps she was right that she could not ally herself with the man who was going to ruin her brother. But it was not as if he was persecuting the family for no reason. What was happening now was the inevitable result of Scofield's actions. He must have known that the truth would come out eventually and it would destroy his family.

If the Duke cared for his sisters as much as Peg claimed he did, he should have taken actions to protect them, when this moment came. He should never have refused the offers for the older girl and should have allowed Peg a Season to find proper suitors of her own. Now, he would be gone, leaving the girls to fend for themselves.

When that happened, Peg would need him.

For a moment, he allowed himself a fantasy of rescue. He would save her and she would be grateful. They would marry, just as he'd hoped. And then reality returned. He might have to rescue her, but she would never forget that he was both the cause of and the solution to her problems. She would grow to hate him for it, if she did not hate him already.

All the same, she could not be serious about ending with him now, without some kind of plan in place. They had lain together. That act, to him, meant a permanent commitment to stay with each other. At least he could not retract his promises until he was sure that no child was going to result from their intimacy. He had vowed to himself that he would never abandon a woman in the position his mother had been left in, to raise a baby without a name.

The upper classes were different. At least, the men were, judging by the example of his father, who seemed neither surprised nor embarrassed by having a son who did not share his surname. But David had thought that a woman like Peg would have been more concerned with the possible consequences than she had been. Could she really be that naive?

Perhaps she had made the decision to lie with him on an incomplete understanding of what was to come, just as she had when deciding to stand by her brother. She might think she could help him through the coming storm. But David was not even sure if ladies were allowed to visit the inmates of Newgate. If they were, they would attract all the wrong sorts of attention.

She was a beautiful young woman and would be fair game for predatory young men who offered help and protection, only to leave her no better than the lovely Miss Devereaux. If she turned out to be enceinte and unmarried, she would have even less protection from scoundrels.

The thought of what awaited her horrified him, as did the knowledge that he had made it even worse by taking her maidenhead. Her dismissal of him had been humiliating, but he would have time to lick those wounds in private at a later date. She might not want him as a lover, but he was not going to allow her to rid herself of him as a friend until he was sure she would be safe alone.

So, with the first light of day, he had sent a letter to the Scofield house, announcing that Mr Castellano had recovered from his illness and would be returning for their next lesson.

Later that morning, he arrived at the front door, pomaded and smiling, fully invested in his old disguise. A servant took him to the music room, where, a short time later, a yawning Peg arrived, obviously still exhausted from the night's activities.

He grinned at her and bowed, every bit the clown that he had pretended to be when he had taken the job.

She glared back at him and whispered, 'Why are you here?'

'We are not through with our lessons yet,' he re-

She looked horrified at being singled out and cast a glance at Hugh that contained all the guilt that he had probably hoped to see.

David gave a slight beckon of his hand to remind her that he was standing before her and needed her attention. 'And what dance do you recommend we do for your brother, my lady? You must be the one to pick a favourite.'

He was giving her the opportunity to pick a dance she knew well, which should save them both from embarrassment. Unfortunately, the girl seemed more panicked than confident in having to make the choice. Thinking for a moment, she said, 'The Boulanger.' She paused, covering her mouth. 'No. We would need to make a circle for that.'

'Not enough people,' he agreed. To give her a hint, he tapped his stick on the floor three times. He could see Peg mouthing the word *waltz*, willing her sister to understand it.

Liv ignored them both and blurted, 'Sauteuse,' which was more a step than an actual dance. Though it was easy enough, it was fast and required that the lady pay attention to where her partner might lead.

'Very well,' David said with a nervous smile, and reached out gingerly to take the older sister by the hands. Then, he began to count for her, this time in English. 'One, two, three.'

But instead of attending to what she was doing, she kept glancing back at her brother in apology or looking to David for approval. Her steps were leaden

minded her. 'I cannot simply disappear without an explanation.'

'Then I will dismiss you,' she said, pointing towards the door.

'Since you did not hire me, I think that action must be left to your brother,' he replied.

'And what action would that be?' They both turned at the interruption to see the Duke standing in the doorway. Lady Olivia was at his side, trying not to look panicked that her usual escape plan might be uncovered.

'Your Grace,' David said with a subservient bow, trying to remember his accent.

'Hugh,' Peg said with an artificially bright smile as if there were no one else she would rather see. 'Why are you not in Parliament?'

'And why were you not in your bed at three o'clock in the morning?' he replied.

For a moment, the Duke was the only one in the room who was not shocked to silence. Then, Peg put her hands on her hips and an outraged expression on her face. 'Are you in the habit of checking our beds at night to see if we occupy them? If so, you have far surpassed normal levels of brotherly concern.'

Scofield laughed. 'I do not have to check your bed when my reading is disturbed by the sound of my little sister sneaking through the kitchen at dawn after returning from God knows where.' He turned to David. 'It strikes me as odd that such spectacular disobedience has only begun since the arrival of our friend the dancing master.'

David responded with an owlish look of confusion, putting his hand to his breast in silent denial.

But Peg would not leave well enough alone. 'Hugh, you are far too suspicious of everyone we come in contact with. Why must it be the dancing master that corrupted us?'

'*Corrupted* is a rather strong word,' David added, though there was no sign that anyone in the Bethune family wanted his opinion.

'If he is not at fault, then surely you must be ready to demonstrate the dances he has taught you,' Scofield said, gesturing towards the centre of the room.

'Now?' Peg said, obviously horrified.

'I told you that there would be a test of your skills,' he added with a tight smile.

'You said we would have a month,' Peg reminded him.

'But it seems that I already need proof that this is a productive activity and not some devious scheme to escape this house. And do not think the pause in dance lessons and your sudden interest in Bond Street has gone unnoticed, either.'

He must have spoken to his men and was aware that his sisters had spent the last two days losing their keepers and moving unescorted through London. David stared at each of them in feigned confusion, doing his best to pretend that he'd had no part in their activities.

'I have no idea what you mean,' Peg replied, her smile overly bright, her mind probably racing to find a way to avoid the inevitable discovery. 'But if you

wish for a demonstration of our dancing, I see no reason why we cannot oblige. I just hope you do not mean to fault Mr Castellano because we are indifferent pupils. He really has done his best. And he has been ill,' she added, as if this would explain everything.

'I hope he is not about to experience a relapse.' Hugh turned to stare at David with a look that would have convinced a weaker man to run for the door.

David showed no concern in response, answering with a subservient bow of his head. 'I am much better now. And the ladies should not think so little of their abilities. They are both most talented.'

'I am well aware of that,' Hugh replied. 'But I have no idea if those skills extend to dancing.'

'How do you expect us to show you, without music?' Peg interrupted, stalling for time.

'I expect you to do it the same way you have been Hugh countered. 'The servants say they hear mu conversation coming from the room and occasio long silences. But they have not heard a single n of music.'

'It is possible to learn the steps by counti David said, tapping his cane on the floor. '*Uno, tre.* Like so.' He gave one of his brilliant smiles t Duke as if the matter should be obvious to any

'*Uno, due, tre,*' the Duke agreed, returning smile with a glare and pointed again at the m shift dance floor.

'Of course,' David said with a deep bow, h out his hand to Lady Olivia.

instead of the sprightly hops required and she could not seem to follow his perfectly even pace.

'Enough,' said Hugh, before they could embarrass themselves more than they already had.

David released her, stepped away and bowed again, then turned to the Duke with a rueful smile, bracing himself for the response.

None came. Instead, he turned to his other sister. 'And what have you learned, Peg?' Scofield's voice was soft, but there was no gentleness to it. Instead, it held unmistakable menace.

David turned to her with another bow, formal and impersonal. 'My lady? A waltz, perhaps?'

'Of course,' she said, stepping forward. He was not sure she had ever done the dance before, but he had, and it was the easiest one he could think of. She had followed where he had led for more than a week. And in bed, she moved like a part of his own body. He was confident that between the two of them, they could show the Duke enough skill that they might salvage this day after all.

Rather than taking her by the hands, he put his hands gently upon her waist. She responded by gripping his shoulders and taking a deep, nervous breath. With a slight inclination of his body, he indicated that they were about to start.

Despite the anger she must still hold for him, she smiled in response and followed his lead. They moved well together, just as he knew they would. Dancing to the rhythm he set was as natural as breathing and he spun her easily about the room, as if they'd spent every minute of their lives practising for just this moment. She was light as a feather in his arms and it made him wish that they'd spent some of the last few days actually dancing so he could have a few more memories like this one.

'Enough!' This time, Hugh shouted, breaking the mood that had filled him while they'd danced. Peg pulled away from him, half turning in an attempt at rejection. But the blush on her face said that she'd enjoyed the waltz far too much to be just another pupil.

David turned to look at the Duke. Scofield's face was dark with fury, his hands balled at his sides. 'Castellano, or whatever you name is. My office. Now!' He stabbed the air with a finger, pointing down the hall towards the study.

And now, David would see what happened to people who crossed the mad Duke of Scofield. He looked back at Peg with a smile, trying to ignore the look of horror on her face at the way their lessons had ended. 'Ladies,' he said, offering a flourish and bow to encompass the pair of them. Then he preceded the Duke out of the room, feeling like a prisoner on the way to the gallows.

When he had set out on this adventure, he had joked to his editor that if the Duke uncovered his ruse, he was likely to be found dead. This was the first moment that he actually thought the prediction might be true. His palms went cold and clammy as he thought of the books in the apartment and the desperate letter that must have evoked the response they'd read. There was an embarrassing hitch in his breathing that he had to struggle to control. This must be what terror felt like, for he had never felt like this before. Nor could he think of a time that he had ever been in this much danger.

Whatever it was, he would not let it unman him. He focused on the corridor in front of him, weighing the possibility of darting away down a side hall or making a run for the front door, all the while feeling the eyes of the Duke focused between his shoulder blades, prodding him forward like the point of a dagger.

He wanted to run. But if he ran, his investigation was over. He would never know what had happened. Now that he had to make the choice of walking into a private room with a murderer or saving his own life, he realised that, if he was to have any peace in life or death, he had to know as much of the truth as he was able to find. The nearness to that truth was all it took to calm his nerves and ready him for the confrontation ahead. He tightened his grip on the walking stick he carried, ready to strike if needed, and continued forward.

When they entered the study, the Duke slammed the door behind them with a thunderous crash that would have turned his knees to jelly had it occurred a few moments before. Then Scofield pushed past him, walking around the desk to throw himself into the chair behind it like a king taking his throne. He stared at David with an intensity that pinned him in place near the door. The silence between them stretched tight as a wire.

When it was clear that David was not about to blurt a confession, the Duke yielded and spoke. 'I told you when I hired you to stay away from my sisters.'

David shrugged and walked forward, closing the distance between them. When he spoke, he did not bother with an accent. 'It is somewhat difficult to teach dancing without making some contact.'

'Do not toy with me!' the Duke snapped. 'It is clear from the way my younger sister looked at you as you danced that there has been more than a little— contact, as you call it.'

David looked back at him without expression, for it was an implication about a lady that no true gentleman should admit to.

The Duke responded with a roar of disgust. 'I knew it was a risk to bring a stranger into the house. I was a fool to allow it, or to think the girl would have better sense. And you…' His finger stabbed the air again, pointing in David's face. 'You dishonourable cur. You—whoever you are. If you had sufficient rank to earn the challenge, I would call you out over this.'

'How interesting that you think only certain people are worth killing face to face,' David replied. He watched the rage simmering in the other man's eyes before adding, 'And my real name is David Castell.'

'The muckraker,' the Duke spat the words.

'Journalist,' David corrected, smiling as though the recognition was meant as a compliment.

'I can guess what you came to find,' the Duke responded. 'You want to write another article tracing all the villainy that has occurred in this country back to my doorstep.'

'The thought had occurred to me,' David replied.

'Do what you will to me,' the Duke replied. 'I do not care one way or the other what is said about me. But only a spineless worm would toy with my sister to gain the information he wanted.'

He had to agree. It would have been a shameful thing to do. 'It was never my intent,' David answered back, then paused, knowing that what he'd said was untrue. He had planned to charm the information out of one or the other of the sisters, using whatever advantages he could. If he had not fallen in love with Peg, he might never have noticed the infamy of his own behaviour.

The Duke scoffed at his weak denial. 'Next you will be telling me that what occurred between you and Margaret was a matter of genuine affection.'

'And suppose it was?' he said, unwilling to deny what he felt. 'Are you ever going to free your sisters from this house and allow them to marry? Or do you mean to drag them down with you when I publish the things I have discovered?'

'My sisters' futures are none of your concern,' Hugh replied, his expression icy. 'Nor do I care about your supposed feelings for Margaret, or whatever happened between you. I only need to be sure that it never happens again and does not become part of one of your sordid articles.'

'I would never...' David said, disgusted at the suggestion.

'Since you entered my house by lying, I have no reason to trust your words.' Scofield pulled out a drawer in front of him and produced a chequebook, then began writing. 'David Castell, with two *l*s? Well, then, Castell, in a few moments, you will be leaving this house never to return. You will not speak to or write a word about either of my sisters, once you have crossed over the threshold.'

'I had no intention of including them in my article,' David replied, knowing that, this time, he was honest. 'It was only you that I was interested in.'

'And supposedly you have found facts that will damn me.' The Duke gave another sceptical cough. 'Then it will surprise you to learn that I do not give a fig about what you might say about me. I cannot think of a crime that has not already been attributed to me. Write whatever you think you know and put an end to this.' He continued to write the cheque, ripping it from the book with an angry snap of his hand and pushing it across the desk.

David picked it up and took a moment to admire the impressive number written on it. The amount was more than enough to tempt even the most unrepentant bounder to leave and not look back. He took it and ripped it neatly in half, setting the pieces back on the desk. 'This will not be necessary.'

'Because you stand upon your honour?' the Duke said, unsmiling. 'Or is it Castellano's honour? Perhaps his is better than yours.'

'Peg has known my name, almost from the first,'

he said. His purpose as well, though he did not want to endanger her by saying so.

'Lady Margaret, to you,' the Duke snapped.

David shook his head. 'To me, she will always be Peg.'

'It does not really matter, because you will never be seeing her again,' the Duke replied.

David tipped his head and raised a finger in warning. 'On that, I am not so sure. You see, Your Grace, I happen to love her. And I suspect she might feel the same. If I discover that to be true, I have no intention of leaving her to suffer under your dubious influence.'

'You find me to be the problem?' Scofield's eyebrows disappeared into his hairline as he rose from his chair in offence.

David stared back at him, unflinching. 'I will not rest until I am sure she is safe. And from what I know of you thus far, I do not believe she is safe with you.'

The Duke slammed his fists down hard on the desktop, probably as a prelude to the beating that David was about to receive. He pointed towards the door. 'Worry about your own safety, Castell. Hers is my concern, not yours. Now get out of this house before I—'

'Kill me?' he interrupted, honestly curious for the response.

'Have you thrown bodily into the street,' the Duke finished.

Compared to his previous crimes, and the things the Duke had threatened before, it was a mild response. Where was the fit of madness? Where was the uncontrollable rage that the letter had described? Since David had been actively trying to provoke him, he'd expected to be engulfed in anger that burned like wildfire. Instead, Scofield's response was amazingly cold.

David stared at him for a moment, wondering if the Duke was the sort of coward who could only pounce once his victim had turned his back. But there was no sign that the other man tensed to strike. If anything, he looked exhausted by his brief display of temper.

When he was sure that there was nothing more to come, David said, 'Very well, I will leave. For now, at least. But I shall return.' Then he deliberately turned his back on a murderer and paused, waiting for the reaction.

'What are you dawdling for?' the Duke snapped. 'Go!'

'As you wish,' David said, turning back and offering the Duke a last smile that he was sure would annoy him. 'Give my regards to Peg.' Then he did as he had been commanded and left the house with much to think about.

Chapter Fourteen

The shouting had not stopped for three-quarters of an hour.

Peg tried not to hope that her sister was receiving the majority of Hugh's anger. It hardly seemed fair that Liv, who had barely been involved in the escapades with David, should be punished for Peg's mistakes.

For herself? Even if she had done wrong, she had meant well. She had only aided David in an attempt to clear her brother. It was not her fault if he was actually guilty. She had trusted him, as a good sister should. If he was truly a madman with uncontrollable urges, she had never seen them. How was she to know that things would end thus?

If she had not been so sure of a positive outcome to their searching, she would not have lain with David. Or perhaps it had never really mattered to her. Perhaps she had suspected from the first how things might end and had grabbed for as much happiness as she could get, before returning home to face the future.

Surprisingly, she regretted nothing of what had happened between them. She had loved David then, and still did, despite the way things had ended. Her only mistake had been in falling in love with a man whose needs were so outside the welfare of her own family that she could not be with him.

It would have been far worse had she fallen for an actual dancing master with a string of foolish young girls and broken hearts behind him. David had not meant to break her heart. He had at least been sincere in his feelings for her. Since it was unlikely that she would ever marry, she was fortunate to have a lost love that she could look back on.

There was a moment of silence and the door to the study opened, revealing her sister, tears staining her white face and a handkerchief clutched in her hand. She looked to Peg and gave a helpless shrug as a sob escaped her and she rushed up the stairs towards her room.

'Next.'

Peg rose from the bench where she'd been sitting and walked into the office. Her brother was staring at her, probably waiting for her to blurt a confession or burst into tears as Olivia had. Instead, she stared back at him, unwilling to yield information he might not already know.

'Explain yourself,' he said at last.

'What have I done, precisely, that needs an explanation?' she replied. 'I danced successfully with the dancing master and proved to you that I have been making good use of my time with him.'

'Good use of your time?' Hugh made a slight gagging noise as if he had guessed exactly what had happened when she was alone with David. 'He was a reporter, not a dancing master. Apparently, you knew that and kept it from me.'

'Because I guessed how you would react,' she said. 'You would have called a halt to the lessons immediately and kept me in ignorance, just as you have been doing since Father died.'

'I have been trying to protect you,' Hugh said softly. 'To keep you safe from people like Castell, who has turned you against your family and taught you things that no innocent girl should know.'

'That is not true,' she insisted. 'I am still a member of this family. I have never left it. But I wanted to know the truth about what has happened in this house and it is clear that you are not going to tell us what it is.'

'You only think you want to know the truth,' he said in a strange voice that was quite different from the commanding ducal tone she was used to. 'Things were better off as they were.'

He might have been right. She could not deny that knowing did put a barrier between them that had not been there before. 'Better for you, perhaps,' she said, not looking away. 'But you cannot keep the rest of us safe from the facts for ever.'

He sighed. 'Perhaps I can't. But for a while, at least, we will go back to how we used to be. Whatever has been going on stops from this moment forward. I have banned Castell from the house and scolded your sister for leaving you alone with him while she pursued that idiot, Clement. You will not be left unchaperoned in the future.'

She greeted this news with silence, still unsure whether it upset her or not. She had already decided to part with David. Since there was no one else she wanted to see, the presence of a chaperon in future hardly mattered to her.

When she did not answer him, he prompted, 'Now, I would like to hear from you.'

'Do you expect me to apologise for something?' she said, tipping her head to the side. 'Because I do not feel the least bit sorry.'

'Foolish child,' he snapped. 'Don't you understand that he used you? No matter what he claimed, he was only trying to get information about this family.'

'About you,' she corrected, pressing her advantage. 'He thinks you are a murderer. I told him it was not true.' She stared back at Hugh. 'Am I right, or not?'

'You are not supposed to ask such questions,' he said.

'That is no answer,' she reminded him, studying the expression on his face. He did not look guilty as much as nervous.

'You should not ask questions like that unless you are sure you will like the answer,' he said.

This was not an encouraging response at all. But there was still something in it that seemed off. 'I know that you reached out to the keeper of an asylum,' she said and watched his nervousness turn to shock. 'Does madness run in our family? I have a right to know that, at least.' Perhaps that was why he was so eager to keep them from marrying. He wanted to prevent the birth of another generation of mad Bethunes.

'Do not concern yourself with that,' he said hurriedly. 'No one is going to an asylum.'

'I gathered that,' she said. 'If it was going to happen, it would be done by now.'

As she had pressed him on the subject, her brother's complexion had gone from red with rage to a chalky white. Now he struggled to regain control of the conversation. 'We are not here to talk about that. We were speaking of your indiscretion with the supposed dancing master.'

'You have nothing to worry about on that account,' she assured him, trying not to feel the ache in her heart. 'When the time came to decide what was most important to me, I chose family, as I always knew I would. Anything that might have existed between Mr Castell and me is over.'

'That is not what he led me to believe,' Hugh said.

'Really?' With that one desperate word, she spoiled any attempt she'd been making to be brave or calm or adult and proved to her brother just how important David was to her.

'But his opinion does not matter,' Hugh reminded her with a cold smile. 'You just said you were finished with him. You will not be seeing him again.

Family is most important to you and your family does not plan on speaking of his business here ever again. Your time with him will be as if it has never happened.'

The way her brother spoke, he expected her to erase the memories from her mind completely, allowing him to write the story he had chosen for them, where there were no murders, no gossip and no one from outside the house coming to spoil his lies with the truth. 'No,' she said, then stopped, surprised at the sound of her own voice.

'No to what, precisely?' he asked, unmoved.

'What if I do not want to pretend that nothing has changed?'

'You are still underage and I am still your guardian. You have little choice in the matter but to do as I say,' he reminded her.

'Your control does not extend to the contents of my mind,' she reminded him. 'Nor can you command my heart not to feel.'

'Your heart,' he scoffed.

'At least I still have one,' she snapped. 'Unlike some people in this house.'

For a moment, she had forgotten the token they had found in his bedroom and the fact that he might be suffering as much, or more, than any of them. But the depth of his suffering was there, in his eyes, just for a moment. Then it was replaced by his usual expression of cold, dictatorial control. 'Your heart and mind are your own. Do as you wish with them as long as they do not lead your body into any more trouble. Do not think you can sneak away and prowl Bond Street unescorted as you have been doing. The careless men that were left to watch you when you went out of the house have been discharged and the next ones will be far more diligent.'

'You cannot keep us imprisoned in this house for ever,' she said.

'Not for ever,' he agreed. 'But your recent behaviour supports my belief that you need to be restrained right now. When you have demonstrated that you will not use your freedom to seek ruin, perhaps I will give it to you. Until that time, we will leave the restrictions in place.' He gestured towards the door to inform her that the interview was at an end.

All in all, she'd have preferred the shouting and tears that her sister's interview had contained. Liv might be crying now, but she would dry her face and she and Alister would find a way to meet, just as they always did.

But she and David would not be so lucky. In their case, her brother had not wasted energy on anger. He had simply removed David from her life and doubled the guard to keep them apart. It had been her intention to do just as Hugh wanted. But now that she had no choice, she felt nothing but regret. The happiest time of her life was over and family obligation demanded that she pretend it had never happened.

David left the Scofield town house strangely, gloriously alive and more confused than he had ever been in his life. He had given the murderous Duke both reason and opportunity to end him. He had even goaded him towards violence.

And the man who was supposedly given to mad fits of homicidal rage had not acted on any of his threats. He had offered money, of all things, signing the cheque in a smooth hand that showed no trace of excess emotion.

For a time, David had expected that one of the Duke's henchmen would follow him out of the house and do the job that the Duke would not. But apparently, he was not even worth that. The guard lounging at the corner of the house followed him only as far as the end of the street before returning to his post.

For a confrontation with a notorious murderer, it had been most disappointing. It made no sense that the man would foster such an air of danger, only to be mild when violence was actually called for. Even David could agree that he deserved a sound beating for seducing the fellow's beloved sister. But there had not been as much as a slap.

There had also been no sign that the Duke feared an exposé on the front page of a newspaper, telling everything that David had learned. He had been completely unperturbed when he'd said, 'I do not care what is said about me.'

David replayed the words in his mind again and again, trying to remember each nuance of the inflection. Had there been the subtlest emphasis on the word *me*? That implied that he would rather the world think he was a murderer than to reveal the actual truth of the matter, that there was someone far more interesting to base the story on.

In any case, the Duke knew more about the matter than he was willing to admit. It was an interesting fact, but not particularly useful, even if David had not been banned from contacting the Scofield family. The interdict on his presence in the house was a minor inconvenience, at best. The only thing he valued inside the house was the woman he loved and it was unlikely that the Duke would have confided the truth to her.

All the same, he wished he could ask her.

And that was barely a half-truth. When he thought of Peg, he wished for many things, the least of which was a chance to talk about her brother. Every moment without her felt as though he was missing some fundamental part of himself and was surviving, rather than living.

He doubted that Scofield meant to keep her chained in her room to prevent further indiscretions. David had but to bide his time and wait until she was allowed out to shop or visit the library. Then he would intercept her and find a way to persuade her that, whether the Duke was guilty or innocent, she could not possibly remain in his house after what they had done together.

There was still the niggling problem that she had informed him she wanted nothing to do with him, ever again. He grinned. If his suspicions after today's interview with the Duke turned out to be true, he might have to concede that she had been right all along. It remained to be seen whether she would still be angry with him if the article he wrote was not about her brother after all.

For now, he needed to review his notes and find another source of information that could confirm or deny the fact that the Duke of Scofield was mad as a March hare. He prayed that today's suspicions were true and the man was not as dangerous as he'd always thought. If Peg had been right all along, he owed her an apology. With it he would offer his hand and his heart. Then he would see if her feelings for him extended beyond a single night.

Chapter Fifteen

Just as Hugh had promised, the next day things were back to normal. Normal for the rest of the family, at least. Olivia was sitting in her chair in the morning room, reading a novel, and pretending that she was not plotting a way to marry Alister and escape her brother, the murderer.

Hugh was in his study, or the library, or some other serious location, doing serious ducal things and pretending that he had not already killed two people and, at any time, might go mad and kill again.

And she…

Peg was newly initiated into the reality that the rest of her family had shared for years. Until a short time ago, she had been floating gently in the illusion that there was nothing wrong with her life other than a few gossipy neighbours and a brother who was far too strict to allow a young girl to have the fun she deserved. She had been an infant, then. Now, she was newborn and growing rapidly into a jaded adult.

Though she had insisted to David that she must stay with them, now that she was here, she could not manage to trust anyone in this house. They'd all lied to her, keeping her in the dark about the social ruin that might fall on them when David, or someone like him, finally uncovered the truth.

When that happened, they would have to see if Alister was really serious enough about Olivia to marry her, no matter what. Peg suspected not. If he was truly enamoured, he'd have married her already. There was already something that prevented him. In Peg's current mood, she suspected it was her own presence that was the problem.

Liv's plan had been a marriage that came complete with a troublesome little sister who would need to be fed and clothed and launched. Alister had always seemed pleasant enough when she'd spoken to him. But there was a certain reserve in his interactions with her that made her wonder if he truly enjoyed her company or was secretly hoping that someone else would marry her so he might never have the responsibility of treating her as family.

If that was true, it was a shame for all of them that she had not run off with David. It would have created a great scandal, but it would have removed an impediment to Liv's future happiness.

That would leave Hugh with no one to care about but himself. It would serve him right. After listening to him deny the family problems and insist that things could ever be *normal*, she was considerably less sorry for him than she had been. Either he had been lying through his teeth and stalling for time, or he did not understand how devastating David's article might be.

And though she did not want to, she missed David, as well. The morning seemed interminably long now that she knew she would not see him. Nor could she sneak out and go to him, for Hugh had been true to his word and hired extra guards around the house to prevent clandestine meetings with Alister and to make sure that the faux dancing master did not attempt to return.

The silence in the house was driving her mad. It was probably for the best that she did not see David again, since his plan to disgrace the family had not changed. But she could not really fault him for it. Her brother deserved the justice he was about to get. As a member of his family, it was her destiny to share in the punishment.

How unfair was it that the only source of hope and comfort she might have through the upcoming troubles would be the man that revealed them to the world? Who would she talk to when the silence of this house became too much to bear? How could she live without the feel of his hand, the touch of his lips, the heat of his body against hers?

And what would she do if the night in bed had created a child? She had been quite sure at the time that a proposal would render such problems moot. Now he was lost to her and she might have to face her foolish mistake alone.

But that had happened when she was sure Hugh

was innocent. Despite what they had found out so far, when she talked to him, there was no sign of hidden madness, or even a bad case of nerves. Could he really have been speaking of a friend when he wrote to the asylum for help?

Maybe there was still something she could find that made the current situation less damning, or at least easier to understand. If David's plan had been to find information inside this house, there was no reason that she could not keep looking on her own. She knew the people in it far better than he did. She might recognise an important detail that he had missed.

She looked to her sister, who was staring out the window, twisting a handkerchief in her hands.

'Olivia, how much do you remember about the night Father died?'

'We do not speak of that night,' her sister said quickly.

'But why do we not?' she countered. 'It is because Hugh will not allow it. And given the rumours circulating around this house, his word may be the last one we can trust.'

'You have always been his staunchest defender,' her sister said, surprised. 'What has changed?'

'Let us say it is more important for me to know the truth than it used to be,' she said. 'Now, tell me what you remember.'

'I was not here for much of it,' she admitted, embarrassed. 'But I remember Father and Hugh arguing at dinner.' She paused. 'I cannot remember the reason for it. But they argued so often back then that I'd got used to ignoring it.'

'And after dinner?' Peg prompted.

'I went to my room and changed. Then I met Alister in the garden,' she replied, with a blush. 'We spoke for a little more than an hour.'

'You talked,' Peg said, with a knowing nod.

'It is not what you think,' Liv said hurriedly. 'He was a perfect gentleman.'

'Of course,' Peg agreed, thinking that Alister would do much better for himself if he were more of a rake and less honour bound. A new thought hit her. 'And when you meet Alister in the garden, why is it that I never hear Caesar barking? It seems that it takes nothing at all to upset that dog to a frenzy.'

'When we are going to be in the garden, I take him a treat so that he does not pester us,' she said. 'Usually a bone from the kitchen. It is enough to keep him occupied for hours.'

That, at least, explained why the dog did not alert the household to an attacker from the yard. He was already too busy with the bone Liv had given him earlier. She made a mental note to tell David, should she ever see him again. 'And what happened after you got back to the house?'

'I went to the library to get a book,' she said. 'I stayed there and read until it was time for bed.' Her brow furrowed as if she was trying to remember. 'At midnight, I think I went to the study to say goodnight to Father.'

'You think?' Peg said, confused.

'Why else would I have gone to the study?' Liv said, as if trying to remember. 'There was a scream. Later, I realised that it was me screaming and not someone else. I was standing over Father's desk, screaming. He was slumped over. I could not see the knife, but there was so much blood...' Her voice trailed away and her eyes went vacant as her mind became trapped in the past.

Peg reached for her, hugging her as her shoulders shuddered with suppressed sobs. When she managed to regain some control, Liv said, 'This is why we do not speak of that night. I found the body. Then Hugh was there, leading me from the room, calling for the housekeeper to give me a brandy.'

'I am sorry that I asked you,' Peg said softly.

But now that she was remembering Liv could not seem to stop talking. 'He was so calm. It was as if he wasn't surprised. He did not look at Father at all. Just at me.'

'You do not have to think about it any more,' Peg assured her. She had given more than enough information already. There was no need for her to dig for more.

Liv's version of events had been very similar to her own. The timing was right, as was the sound of screaming, which she now knew was Liv discovering the body.

She paused, puzzled. Something was almost right, but not exactly right. She closed her eyes, forcing her mind back to that night, trying to remember the details. She had been in her room, reading, when she had been disturbed by the first scream. And that had been what it was: a single, piercing shriek. Then, nothing.

She had got up from the bed and was all the way to the door before the next screams came. That had been a series of cries, lower, longer and more heart-felt. Even in her room, she had known that it was Liv crying out and that something in their lives had changed irrevocably to cause this reaction.

But the first cry was not a voice she'd recognised. Clearly, Liv had been in shock if she'd thought she had been the cause of the first cry. More likely, some-one had found the body, screamed and ran. Liv had heard it and gone to see what the matter was. She had cried out when she'd found their father, her mind blotting out those few moments before the shock and the sound that had disturbed her.

Someone else had been in the study that night. A woman. She had been gone by the time Liv had ar-rived in the room from the library.

But for the moment, Peg had to deal with the chaos she'd created by forcing her sister to relive the most traumatic night of her life. Peg carefully untwined the handkerchief from Liv's hands, shook it out and pressed it to the tears that were still streaming down her face. 'I am sorry for making you talk about this,' she said, giving her older sister another hug.

'Then why did you?' Liv demanded. 'The only way I am able to function at all in this madhouse is to ignore what happened in it and pretend that I did not see the horror in the study that night.'

'Because I need to know,' Peg whispered, wondering if her sister could understand. 'Both of you have managed to keep me in the dark about it. I know you were trying to protect me, but I am a grown woman and old enough to know the truth.' She gave Liv yet another hug and an encouraging smile. 'Now, at least, I can share your burden with you and make it lighter.'

Liv shook her head. 'Your efforts to uncover the facts with Mr Castell have only made the problem larger. Now, Hugh will never let us out of his sight. We will be trapped here for ever. And I cannot stand it much longer. Why could you not have left well enough alone?' She pushed her fist against her mouth, as if she regretted speaking a thing she'd meant to keep secret.

Peg pulled back, shocked. Perhaps she had grown too used to her favoured status as the baby of the family. If she meant to behave as an adult, she must accept responsibility for the trouble she had caused her sister. She reached out to take Liv's hand again. 'I am sorry. But I will find a way to make things right again.'

Liv rose, pulling away from her. 'Things were never right, Margaret, and they have only got worse. Please, for both our sakes, stop trying to fix this.' Her sister left the room, shoulders stiff as if she could no longer stand to share the space with her.

Peg sat for a moment, trying to relive the last few minutes, to glean every detail from them. Perhaps some part of David's zeal had rubbed off on her. In retrospect, she was not nearly so bothered by Liv's anger as she should have been. Instead, she could not stop thinking about the other woman who had been in the study before Liv. Who could it have been?

She went down the hall and paced out the distance between the rooms in question, ending in the study which was, thankfully, unoccupied. Assuming that Liv had put down her book in the library and had run to the study, it would have taken less than half a minute to arrive. It would have been awfully hard for the woman in the room to get away without running past her in the hall, or at least being seen.

Then she remembered the open window behind the desk. It was the quickest way out of the room and the only one that could guarantee leaving without running into a member of the family or staff. Considering the fuss that Liv had made when discovering the body, no one would have thought to search the grounds for some time. Someone in the back garden would have been able to leave through the gate, or return to the house by the kitchen door undetected.

She sat down in her brother's chair for a moment, thinking. Would a woman have had the strength to kill their father? Or was she just present when the murder had happened? If she had witnessed something, it would have explained the scream. Or had she discovered the body? If she was someone that belonged in the house, a maid or housekeeper, there would have been no reason to run away. More likely she would have been screaming for help.

This meant that a stranger had been in the room when her father had died, or shortly after.

'Is there a reason you are using my desk?' her brother said from the doorway.

Her reverie broken, she looked up at him in surprise. 'I was just thinking.'

'In my office,' he said. 'And what, precisely, would you be thinking about?'

'The night Father died,' she said. At this point, there was nothing to lose by honesty.

'I would rather that you not dwell on the past,' he said.

She shrugged. 'I know you do not like to talk about it. But there are things I want to know.'

He sighed and sat down in the chair in front of the desk. 'There are things many people want to know about that night. I do not know if it is in anyone's power to find the answers.'

That was his first lie, for she was sure he knew the truth, even if he did not want to speak of it. 'I only want to know how you remember it,' she said.

'I heard Olivia scream and I came down the hall to the study, and found her there, standing over the body,' he said. 'She was obviously in shock, so I went out into the hall and shouted for a footman. Then I pulled her from the room.'

'Where were you when you heard the scream?' she asked, leaning over the desk to search his face as he responded.

'In the library,' he said without blinking.

That could not have been right, either. If he had been there, he would have seen Liv before she went to the study, or she would have mentioned seeing him. It was another obvious lie and Peg did not know what to do with it. 'Were you there all evening?' she asked at last, hoping he would tell her that he had just arrived.

'Since supper,' he said.

'And at supper, you argued with Father,' she reminded him.

'It is not something I was proud of,' he said. 'But, yes, we argued on the last night of his life.'

'And you said you would have all of his money, once he was gone,' she reminded him.

He frowned. 'I said many stupid things to him when he was alive. I regret many of them.'

'But not all?' she said.

'He was a very difficult man,' Hugh said with another sigh. 'Now that I have sat in his chair, I understand him better than I did and know he had our best interests at heart. But that did not keep him from being wrong. He was miserly and dictatorial, and I was a fully grown man who did not want to be treated like a schoolboy.'

She had to bite her tongue to keep from reminding him that his sisters were now both fully grown as well and did not need him to behave to them as their father had treated him. 'Were you sad when he died?' she asked, trying another tack.

'That is a hard question to answer,' he replied. 'I remember that it was easier not to focus on what had happened. I summoned the Runners, told the servants to search the grounds, made sure that both of you were safely in your rooms. It was not for some days that things were quiet enough to give the matter thought and, by then, I had got over the initial shock.'

'But once that happened, did you miss him?' she asked.

'There were many things we should have talked about, before I became Duke of Scofield,' he said. 'There are still times I wish I could ask his advice. But regret serves no purpose.'

It was not much of an answer, but it was all she was going to get. He looked at her, searching. 'And what of you? Did you grieve for our father?'

She considered. 'When he was alive, I feared him more than I loved him. But he did not require that I love him. I was in awe and that seemed sufficient for him. When he was gone?' She searched again for a word to describe the feeling. 'I was frightened, more than I was sad. But then you became Duke and I was not scared any more.' At least, not until she had learned he'd been lying to her.

For his part, he seemed satisfied with her answer. 'He was not an easy man to love,' he replied. 'I am sorry if I follow in his footsteps in regard to you and your sister. But I mean what is best for you and hope that, some day, you will understand.' He rose from his chair and looked at her with a raised eyebrow. 'And now, if you don't mind, I would like the use of my study.'

'Of course,' she said, hopping out of the seat she'd forgotten she had usurped. 'I will leave you to your business, then.'

He nodded and she felt the distance widen between them as he changed from being her big brother to a duke who had no time for interruptions.

She left the study, even more confused than she had been when she went to it. It appeared that there had been a strange female in the house on the night of the murder. It also appeared that her brother could not account for his actions at the time the crime occurred. Wherever he had been, it had not been in the library, reading a book.

But there was one person in the house who always knew more than she told. Being the younger daughter and not the lady of the house, Peg had barely spoken to her at all. Perhaps now was the time for that to change.

She returned to the morning room and rang for the housekeeper, doing her best to act like a proper lady and not just the youngest member of the family, whose wishes could be ignored by both family and staff.

By the time Mrs Gates arrived, Peg had taken a seat by the window and she greeted the woman with a firm, superior smile.

'Lady Margaret?' the housekeeper responded with a look of surprise. 'Is there something I might help you with? A biscuit, perhaps, or a cup of tea?'

She shook her head. 'I was just curious about something and hope you might be able to answer a few questions.'

'Of course,' the woman replied, probably thinking it was about a menu or a maid. 'What is it you wish to know?'

'What do you remember of the night my father died?' she asked and watched the housekeeper go white.

'We should not be speaking of such things,' the woman said, glancing at the door as if she was afraid of being overheard.

'I promise you will not get into any trouble for talking to me,' she said with a reassuring gesture. 'If you are worried about the Duke, do not. I have already spoken to him.' Not precisely about questioning the staff, but that did not need to be discussed at the moment.

The housekeeper drew a nervous breath and said, 'Very well, if you have spoken to His Grace about it. But there is not that much to tell. I was in the kitchen going over accounts all evening. I had no idea what had happened until your brother summoned us upstairs to take care of you and your sister.'

This was disappointing. 'You heard nothing out of the ordinary, for the rest of the evening?'

The woman blinked. 'Nothing unexpected.'

Now *this* was an interesting answer. It seemed to say that she was accustomed to unusual things happening in the house and was equally accustomed to ignoring them.

'I already know that Liv met with Alister in the garden,' she said and watched the woman relax a little as one of her secrets was exposed. 'I am interested in the other woman that was in the house that night.'

At this, the housekeeper gasped. 'No one was supposed to know about that.'

'As I said, I have spoken to my brother,' she said, smiling to herself as the housekeeper jumped to yet another conclusion and assumed that Peg knew most of the details already. 'What was happening was really no secret. Please tell me what you remember of it.'

The woman shook her head as if she wished to forget the whole thing, then sighed and spoke. 'The woman came in by the kitchen door as she did whenever she visited.'

'Had she been there many times before?' Peg asked, trying not to look surprised.

The housekeeper considered for a moment. 'Several times over the month leading up to the… incident.' She did not want to say *murder*, but then, who in the family did?

'What did she look like?'

'She was always cloaked and veiled. I could see little of her other than that she was on the tall side and could afford expensive cloth for her cloak.'

'And what happened to her, once she was in the house?' Peg said eagerly.

'Lord Hugh met her and escorted her up the servants' stairs to the second floor.'

This was interesting. It explained the obvious lie about the library, since her brother could not very well tell her he had been entertaining a lady in his room. 'How long did she stay?'

'On that night, I do not know. Things were all a muddle with all kinds of strangers coming and going from the house. But on other nights, she was always gone by three or four in the morning.'

'And did she ever visit again?' Peg asked, suspecting the answer.

'No,' the housekeeper replied. 'Once Lord Hugh became His Grace the Duke, he had no more time for such nonsense.'

'Of course,' Peg agreed. It was either that, or he suddenly had the means to acquire a convenient apartment to entertain ladies who could not enter through the front door. She gave the housekeeper a brilliant smile. 'That is all I wanted to know, Mrs Gates. Thank you so much for your help.'

The woman gave her a confused look before dropping a curtsy and returning to her duties, leaving Peg alone with much to think about. On the night of the murder, Hugh had been entertaining a woman in his room. It was obviously not Miss Devereaux, since she had not been Hugh's favourite at the time of Father's death. It was someone Hugh was willing to lie to protect. And it must have been a serious relationship, if he was willing to let people think him a murderer rather than admit what he had been doing.

A lady. He had been entertaining a gentle-born woman in his room. But if that was true, why had he not married her? He had shown no sign that he was interested in marriage, either before or after the death of their father. What had happened to her? And what might she know about the murder?

Chapter Sixteen

The next morning, Peg stared at her bedroom wall, mourning the loss of David Castell. She was quite sure that given the evidence she had recently gathered, she could prove him wrong about the murder of their father. If he was wrong about that, why not about the other murder?

If he was wrong about both, there could be no damning article about the family to spread across the front page of a newspaper. She could have her old life back without fear of impending disaster, just as her brother had wanted. In time, the gossip about Hugh would die down and he would give her a Season, just as she had wanted from the first.

Or, she could do as she truly wished and spend her life with the man she loved. If the promises he'd made in bed had been true and not just loose talk meant to seduce her... If she was brave enough to be the woman she had told him she was... If she could convince her brother that she had to follow her heart... If her brother would allow her out of the house at all...

There were so many ifs in the future she wanted. The biggest of them was Hugh, who was set against her marrying anyone. She doubted he would be happy to find that she had made her choice, and it was not to be a gentleman from an appropriate family who had been vetted and approved in advance. He would be absolutely livid to hear that the only man she wanted was the muckraker he had banned from the house.

For some reason, the thought of how angry he would be made her smile. She was done with being an obedient little girl who followed his rules no matter how nonsensical they might be. She would do as she pleased and tell him afterwards. The less Hugh knew about her plans for the future, the easier it would be for all concerned. He had his own idea about how things should go and it seemed to make him so happy that she did not want to spoil his good mood before she had to.

But that still left the question of how to get around the obstacles he had set between her and freedom. There was no way to write a letter to David without it being intercepted. Hugh had told the servants to remove anything she added to the family post, so he might examine it for suspicious directions. She could not sneak out of the house. The front door was always guarded and he had hired an additional man to watch the back, to prevent garden meetings with Alister and midnight carriage rides by Peg. If he had his way, she and Liv would not have a moment's freedom until they were proper spinsters who had no hope of their own homes and lives.

None of that mattered. She would find a way to escape the house, no matter how long it took. If she could not have David, she was willing to put all future plans for marriage aside. Nothing could equal what she had already found.

Why had she not told him so, when she'd had the chance? The right time to speak had been immediately after he had professed his love, to assure him that she felt as he did. But then she'd thought there would be more time. She had basked in his words as if they were a warm bath, soaking them in through her skin, answering them with her body instead of speaking the truth plainly. Then, only a few minutes later, everything had changed and it was too late.

She had not wanted to love a man who put her family at risk. Logic told her that a future between them was impossible. But, despite that fact, her heart had leapt in her chest when he'd appeared the next day for a lesson and again when Hugh had spoken of the feelings he'd expressed for her.

She had to believe that those feelings would hold true long enough for her to see him again and explain. Even if, in the end, Hugh would not let her go to him, David had to hear from her lips that it was not just some game she had been playing. Their night together had meant everything to her.

Suddenly, Liv appeared in the doorway, an expression of amazement on her face. 'Have you looked out of your bedroom window this morning?'

Peg rolled her eyes and kicked at the covers, still not wanting to get out of bed. 'There is nothing to

see out there that I have not seen a hundred times.
Unless it is to look at the man watching the garden
gate to keep us from leaving.'

'There is something new this morning,' Liv said.
'And it must be seen to be believed.'

Peg rose with a huff and reached for her wrapper
before going to stand in the window and look down.
'I see nothing unusual.'

'Wait,' her sister said, holding up a hand. 'It will
be passing again in a moment.' She pointed down
the street to a coach rounding the corner and head-
ing down the street to pass their house.

Peg glanced at her sister, who still seemed to be
fixated on the approaching carriage. Then she looked
down herself and saw the sign on the vehicle's roof.

Bond Street. 1:00

'It is very ingenious,' Liv said, smiling. 'The
guards might be suspicious of the carriage, but they
cannot see the message from the ground.'

'And Hugh's bedroom faces the front of the house,'
Peg said with a smile. 'He is unlikely to see it at all.'
She glanced at her sister. 'Who do you think it is for?'

'You, of course,' her sister said with a sigh. 'Unfortunately, I do not think Alister is quite so ingenious.'

'We must go, of course,' said Peg, grinning.

'We?' Liv said with a sigh.

'To leave the house separately will be far too suspicious. We must go shopping and take a maid as chaperon to put Hugh and his guards at ease.'

'I will get in more trouble if this is discovered,' Liv replied. 'At this rate, I will never see Alister again.'

'He will find his way to you, just as David has done to me,' Peg assured her with a softer smile. If he did not, Alister was not worthy of her sister's affection, any more than Richard Sterling had been. In either case, they would be going to Bond Street that afternoon, so she could talk to David.

A little before one, they set out on their highly supervised shopping trip with a maid in tow, two men following a distance behind and a final warning from their brother that there should be no more nonsense or he would lock them in their rooms. It made her wonder just how David hoped to communicate with her. He might still have the key to the *pied-à-terre*, but she had no way to get there without him and no method to signal him that she had come this far.

But as she and her sister were staring into the window of a milliner's shop, she was caught by the reflection of the street behind her and a man on the opposite side, looking in her direction.

She looked once, then twice at the man standing on the street. She was sure that she had not met him before, for she'd have remembered the bright red hair creeping out from under his hat and the monocle clenched in his left eye. Still, there was something vaguely familiar about him. Then, very deliberately, he stared at her and winked with his good eye.

David.

He was disguised again, but it was definitely him. She was so excited by the knowledge that she almost called his name out loud before remembering that her brother's men were watching and would put an immediate stop to any attempt to speak with a stranger.

As she watched, he turned away from her and walked deliberately to a shop on the corner, giving her a final look before disappearing inside.

She tugged Olivia's sleeve. 'Let us cross the street at the next corner. I would like very much to visit the little bookshop there.'

Liv rolled her eyes. 'A bookshop. This is a first from you. But who am I to complain if you finally want to better your mind?' They crossed the street together and entered the shop.

It took a moment for her eyes to adjust to the dimness inside and to see David leaning over a table of books at the back of the store. She worked her way to him in the most uninterested way possible, every nerve of her body on alert at the thought of being near him. Though they had been apart less than a week, it felt like an age.

He leaned his head close to hers and spoke, his lips barely moving. 'I have to see you.'

'And I you,' she said. 'I have news.'

'As do I. And I need your help.'

'Where? How? When?'

'Now,' he said.

Her attempts at hiding her surprise failed dismally as her head snapped up to stare at him.

'Come away with me,' he said, loud enough so there could be no doubt of what he had said. 'Right now.'

She glanced back at her sister and their maid, too focused on a shelf at the front of the shop to notice what she was doing. 'Where are we going?' she asked.

'I am going to Newcastle upon Tyne, to find out what was in the Duke's letter,' he said, his monocle dropping from his eye. 'It is the one place we can get the details on the letter we found in the apartment. The question is, are you coming with me?'

He was not talking about a jaunt across town. The trip north would take several days. If anyone heard of the trip, her reputation would be in tatters and she would have little choice but to beg him for marriage, whether he wanted her or not.

And if, despite what she had found, he proved her wrong again, he would still write his article as planned. Then she would have no reputation to speak of, either. Running away now would not make things any worse.

But, most importantly, she wanted to go with him, to follow wherever he led. No matter the future, things could be as they had been, for just a few days longer.

'Give me a moment,' she said, walking back to her sister.

Once she had Olivia's attention, she pulled her

away from the maid so they could speak privately and whispered, 'I need your help.'

'If you wish me to recommend a book...' She held one out to Peg. 'Take this one so we can be on our way.'

'I am leaving,' Peg said, waving the book aside. 'I need you to give me some time.'

'Leaving?' Liv stared at her in confusion. 'What—?'

Peg held up her hand to stop the questions. 'Do not leave this shop for the next fifteen minutes. When you go, proceed up Bond Street as if nothing has changed until Hugh's men stop you. When they do, you must know nothing, so I will tell you nothing.' She gave her sister's hand a quick squeeze. Then, ignoring Liv's horrified look, she went to the back of the shop and followed David out a rear entry and into a storeroom.

'We have a quarter of an hour before they begin to look for us,' she said as he led her quickly out a door and down a side street.

'More than enough time,' he assured her, trotting to a corner and whistling for a cab. When one arrived, he grabbed her hand and helped her up and into a seat before murmuring directions to the driver.

When they had settled down and were on their way, she looked at him, breathless. 'Now that we are alone, can you tell me what, exactly, we are doing?'

'As I said before, we need to find out what it was the Duke asked that doctor. He is far more likely to talk to you, a member of the Duke's family, than he is to me.' His tone was distant, holding none of the warmth she'd heard in it during their night together.

'Oh,' she said, crestfallen. She'd had hopes that he missed her as much as she missed him. Instead, it seemed he needed to use her to get more information for his story, just as he had used her from the first.

'This trip will not be necessary,' she said, putting on a brave smile to hide her hurt. 'I have talked to everyone in the house and have learned that there was another person visiting us the night Father died. A woman. She was with Hugh, in his room. She was also in the study. Her scream alerted the family to the presence of the body.'

David blinked at her in response. 'How could she be in both the bedroom and the study? Was Scofield with her when the body was found? Or was she with him when he killed his father? That could have been what made her scream.'

'I do not think so,' she replied. It was true, she did not. But it was clear that the evidence she thought definitive was not yet enough to persuade him.

He gave her a sceptical look, as if her information proved nothing at all to him, then continued, 'It is definitely interesting that there was a stranger in the house that night. I am willing to consider the possibility of your brother's innocence, but not enough to trust him with your life. We are going to the asylum in Newcastle so you can speak to the doctor yourself. Once there, he will either exonerate your brother or explain to you how dangerous he actually is.'

'You are still trying to change my mind,' she said, surprised.

He reached out to grab her hand, then stopped before touching her. 'I am trying to protect you. You will not believe me when I say that there is a problem, but perhaps you will take a medical man more seriously. At the very least, your brother's domineering behaviour towards you and you sister borders on obsession. If it should turn out that he is mad and cannot control himself, you are not safe with him.'

It was good to know that he still cared, but it meant nothing without a further commitment. 'What happens if you convince me it is not safe to go home?' she asked, holding her breath.

'I will think of something,' he said. 'I will help you towards whatever future you choose, as long as I am sure you are not under the thumb of a madman.'

Perhaps he did not understand the truth of a woman alone in the world. But if she was not someone's wife or her brother's sister, she was not anyone. She would have no friends, no family and no references to get what limited employment was available to an educated woman. Perhaps he could forge her something, as he had done for himself when getting the job as her dancing teacher.

Or perhaps he could do the obvious thing and marry her. But it was not the thing for the lady to ask the gentleman a question like that. The fact that she had given him the ultimate gift should have been an incentive. Of course, she had told him afterwards that she'd wanted nothing more to do with him. If he was not quick to admit his feelings, she was to blame for it. 'And are you still planning to publish your article?' she asked.

'Let us not talk about that until after we have spoken with the physician,' he said.

'Now you are stalling,' she replied. But it was a better response than he had given her before. The last time, there had been no doubt at all.

'If you do not like my answer, we can turn back,' he said. 'We still have a few moments to return you to the bookshop before you have been missed.'

'No,' she said, wishing that her voice did not sound so hesitant. 'Do not take me back. Let us go to Newcastle and get the answer you are seeking.' If she was honest, she wanted to know as much as he did. She was tired of answering doubts about her family, tired of being lied to by her brother and exhausted by the way each new revelation seemed to contradict the last.

The only thing she was sure of was that she did not want to leave David a moment before she had to. If he wanted to wait until the end of the trip to make his decision, she would at least have a few more hours to pretend that things might work out between them. So she leaned back into the squabs and counted the money in her reticule, hoping that it would be enough to provide any necessities she might want for a journey of several days.

They changed carriages twice before reaching the edge of the city, then rented a plain coach and driver from a small and hopefully reputable stable on one of the lesser-used north roads. 'If Scofield wants to follow us, I have a good idea where he will look,' David said with a smile. 'We will make a point of being elsewhere.'

He did not tell her that her brother would be researching the fastest routes to Gretna Green, since he was still not sure that she was ready to hear it. When she had asked his plans for her after this was over, he had thought of the small ring in his pocket and lost the nerve to speak.

When he was with her, she was his sweet Peg, the light of his life. But while they were apart, he had begun to think of her as Lady Margaret Bethune, a woman miles above him in wealth and status. Even without her brother working actively against her chances at marriage, she could do far better than an itinerant journalist who had been born on the wrong side of the blanket.

Though they'd made love, she'd told him after, in no uncertain terms, that, if forced to choose, she would keep the life she had, even as it fell apart around her.

He could not really blame her for it. But that did not change his feelings for her. For hours, she had been sitting across the carriage from him, staring out the window in silence, as if she found the scenery far more interesting than his company. Or perhaps she was watching the sun set and wondering what would happen when they had to stop for the night.

He had been wondering that, as well. He hoped

that there would be two rooms available to remove the possibility of temptation from their stay. But when they stopped at the coaching inn, he was informed that he and his 'wife' could have the last one available.

It was some consolation that the hosteler did not wink when he declared them married. It allowed them the dignity of pretending that nothing was improper. Peg stood a way off, drinking the brandy and hot water that the tavern maid had given her, ignoring the negotiations until they were through. She turned back to David with a hopeful smile.

'Our room is ready,' he said, watching her carefully to see if the singular nature of the word shocked her in any way.

She blinked once and then gave him a relieved smile. 'Excellent news. I am very tired.' She stepped forward and allowed herself to be led up the stairs by him.

When he had her safely inside the room with the door shut, he blurted, 'I will sleep on the floor.'

'Why?'

The single word stunned him to silence. It could not possibly be the offer he thought it was.

'Is there some problem with your back?' she said, sitting on the edge of the mattress and bouncing once. 'This feels quite comfortable, compared to some beds I have had while travelling. And it is certainly large enough for two.'

'I am taking the floor because, after the way we parted when last we were alone, I did not think you would want to share it with me,' he replied, laying it out plainly for her.

'We did not part under the best circumstances,' she agreed. 'And I am not sure that anything has changed in that. But I have ruined my reputation by running away with you and I doubt that it matters what I do next.' She gave him an inviting smile.

It was what he'd hoped to see, but her words ruined it. 'If it no longer matters what you do with your life, than it is no compliment that you want to share a bed with me,' he replied, ripping off his cravat and throwing it over the back of the nearest chair.

'That is not what I meant,' she said, giving a frustrated tug at her gown. 'It is just that...' she tugged again, trying and failing to reach the hooks '... I did not want to seem missish. We have already lain together. I did not want to seem shocked that you might wish to do it again. But, apparently, I am now being too worldly to appeal to you.'

'That is not true,' he said.

'I assumed you found it as pleasurable as I did. But if you did not...' She gave a final pull at the back of her gown and then gave up and laid down on the bed, prepared to sleep in her clothes.

He sighed and went to her, helping her back up so he could sit on the bed behind her. Then he loosened her gown and stays, so she might sleep comfortably. Once he had started undressing her, he could not resist the opportunity to push her garments down her shoulders and lay his palm flat on the bare skin of her back. 'Do you regret what we did together before?'

'No,' she said, almost too quickly. 'I know it was wrong. But I cannot bring myself to be sorry about it.'

He moved his hand slowly, up and down her back, lost for a moment in the smoothness of her skin. Then he asked, 'What would you do if you didn't have to worry about the future?'

Without another word, she turned to kiss him, her loosened gown bundling between them as he took her in his arms. She whispered against his lips, 'I want to be with you.'

It was all the invitation he needed.

Chapter Seventeen

Peg Bethune was almost exactly where she wanted to be.

First, they were on their way to get information that might lead to the truth of what had happened to her father. There was still a chance that Hugh was innocent and David would not publish. If that was true, there was still hope they could be together in the future.

Second, they were halfway to Gretna Green. If she was honest with herself, she was already ruined and there was only one way to make it right. When they had been together in her brother's apartment, David had proclaimed his love for her. Surely, if the situation was right, a proposal of marriage would be forthcoming.

Last, and most importantly, she was with David and they were alone for the whole night. She could not stop thinking of the brief time spent in the bedroom of her brother's apartment and the wonderous

sensations she had experienced. If that was what con-
stituted a fall from grace, then virtue had been highly
overrated and she was glad she had rid herself of it.

The situation was definitely right for a repeat of
their last meeting. Her gown was open and his hands
had slid under her shift to stroke the skin of her back.
'You said in the apartment that you wanted to see all
of me,' she reminded him, holding her breath and
hoping he remembered.

'I did,' he agreed.

She stood for a moment and stepped out of her
shoes as she shook herself free of the opened gown,
letting it fall to the floor along with petticoat and
stays. After taking a deep breath to steady her nerves,
she pulled her shift over her head and dropped it
with the rest, leaving her in nothing but stockings
and garters.

His gaze raked down her body, heating the skin
wherever it lingered. Then he held up his hand to stop
her as she reached for a garter. 'Leave one mystery
remaining. I will have time to uncover it later.' He
shrugged out of his coat and reached for the buttons
on his breeches.

She watched in amazement as he stripped out
of his clothes until he stood before her, unabash-
edly naked. When they were together before, she
had not had the nerve to look at him. But now there
was so much to see that she could not look away.
He had a broad chest, strong arms and lean, well-
muscled flanks. The plains and hollows of his body
were sharply delineated in the glow of the bedside

candles. And between his legs, in a cloud of hair, his manhood was already hard and growing harder as he stared at her body.

He gave her one more lingering look before closing the distance between them and taking her in his arms. She jerked in shock as skin touched skin and he backed away, raising his arms.

'No,' she said hurriedly, reaching for him. 'It is all right. It was just…' For a moment, it had been too wonderful to stand. She stepped into his arms again, giving a slight shimmy as the length of their bodies touched. She relaxed into the feeling with a sigh.

He laughed and kissed her, his tongue taking her mouth in slow, deep strokes as his hands ran down the length of her back. She responded the same way, tasting his mouth and smoothing her hands down to the dip in his waist and the round muscles beneath it.

The sensation of touching him and being touched by him was intoxicating and she could not seem to get enough of it. Then one of his hands came up to squeeze her breasts and took her to yet another level of desire.

'This is what I should have given you from the first,' he whispered. 'This is what you deserve, every minute of every day. This and so much more.' He scooped her easily into his arms and carried her the last few feet to the bed, dropping to the mattress with her and rolling to the middle. He kissed her again, on the mouth, on the throat and lower. She kissed his shoulder, urging him on until he worshipped her breasts with his tongue, sucking each of them until the flesh was tight and sensitive. Then his fingertips took the place of his tongue, playing with her nipples as his mouth moved lower.

Her fists balled in the sheets as his tongue found her pleasure and, for a moment, her body fought the onslaught of sweetness, back arching, hips rocking from side to side searching for escape. Then she surrendered to it. She released the cloth she held and twined her fingers in his hair to urge him deeper, riding the waves of passion he created until she collapsed, spent.

'Not yet,' he said, kissing the inside of her thigh. He rolled on to his back and made a coaxing gesture with one finger. When she didn't immediately respond, he patted his thighs and held out his arms to her. 'We are not finished. Come to me.'

She straddled his legs, lower at first. Then she slid forward on to his erection, letting it glide into the centre of her, filling her. She rubbed the place where they were joined, intrigued.

He sucked in a breath of air, his body tense. 'Touch wherever you want. Move however you want. Let me feel you.'

She moved slowly at first, then faster, trying to remember the way he had thrust the last time they were together. She gave in to her own feelings, tightening her muscles, holding him inside her as she rode him. She touched herself where he had kissed her, then stroked the inside of his thighs, gripping to steady herself as her pace increased, knuckles brushing against his bollocks, a place she had yet to explore.

When she found her rhythm, she felt him moving under her, withdrawing only to thrust to meet her. The rest of his body seemed to grow as hard as his member, muscles priming for climax. As she felt him release, she drew a finger up to her own body, bringing joy to herself, trembling as he shook, crying out his name as he moaned hers.

She collapsed on to him as he had once done to her, allowing herself a breathless giggle before kissing his ear. What did one say at a moment like this? She settled on 'Thank you' since it only seemed polite.

He gave an exasperated sigh. 'You're welcome, I suppose.' He kissed her neck, shaking his head.

'I do not know the etiquette for such moments,' she said, a little indignant.

'There is none,' he replied, 'other than to follow your heart.'

She raised her head and gave him a sleepy smile. 'My heart brought me here, to you.'

He smiled back. 'I am glad.' He drew the blankets over them, settling down to sleep. 'We can discuss bedroom manners, tomorrow. We must make an early start. But there is still one more night on the road until we reach Newcastle.'

'Another night,' she marvelled.

'And we will not waste a moment of it,' he promised.

Chapter Eighteen

The Hospital for Lunatics at Newcastle upon Tyne was further than he'd planned to go to gather information on Scofield and, now that he could see it, he regretted his plan to bring Peg. It did not look like the sort of place that one brought a lady of any kind, much less the girl that one wished to marry.

As the carriage passed through the heavy iron gates and rolled towards the hospital proper, he could feel the despair hanging like a miasma over the grounds. Peg must have felt it as well for she shrank closer to him on the seat, shivering against his side.

'I understand if you do not want to come in,' he said, eyeing the coachman who had opened the door for them. 'You can wait here, if you wish.'

She took a deep breath and let it out in a resigned sigh. 'I have come too far not to hear the truth with my own ears. As you said from the first, you may need me to persuade the doctor to speak.'

'It will be easier to have a member of the family present,' he agreed, feeling guilty that he even needed her help. It might have been different had he not been asking about a duke. But when questioned about such an august member of society, it was hard to believe that the doctor would be free with his information if he had no incentive to talk other than to satisfy David's curiosity.

They got out of the carriage together and entered a building that was almost as grim on the inside as it had been on the outside. Walls that had once been a pristine white were greyed with years of grime and there was a strange, lingering odour of mildew, burned food and unwashed humanity.

If the entry hall was bad, the rest of the place was most certainly worse. He turned to Peg again, ready to send her back to the safety of the carriage.

Before he could speak, she stepped forward, looked up into the stern face of one of the guards stationed by the door and said, with no trace of fear, 'We would like to see Dr Phineas Dial, please.'

'What's your reason?' the man snapped back at her, in a voice meant to intimidate her into silence.

'That is none of your business,' she said, staring back at him as if he was a speck of mud on her boot. 'You may tell him that his visitor is Lady Margaret Bethune, sister of the Duke of Scofield.' Then she dabbed at her nose with a handkerchief as if offended by the smell. 'Show us to his office, or to a sitting room of some kind. I am not accustomed to being kept waiting in a common hallway.'

David tried not to start in surprise as the orderly

snapped to attention and ran to arrange the meeting she requested. He had forgotten that the woman next to him, his dear, sweet Peg, was also a child of the peerage. She was not likely to be cowed by a person who was socially miles beneath her, even though physically he was a foot taller and twice as wide.

He leaned his head in her direction. 'Very impressive.'

She blinked at him, innocent and unassuming. 'One does not live in Scofield House without learning a few of its tricks.'

'But I have never seen you use them before,' he said, grinning.

She blinked again. 'Do you wish me to stop?'

'On the contrary, I wish you to continue.' This was not the place to tell her that her assertiveness was arousing, but he had hopes that in the future they would have more than enough time to explore it.

The attendant reappeared and led them down a hall to an office on the far end of the wing, opening the door and announcing them to the man who stood respectfully behind the desk to greet them.

'Doctor Dial?' David said with a bow and received a brief nod in response. He offered their cards.

The doctor examined his card and the more ornate card of Lady Margaret Bethune. His reticence dropped away, replaced by fawning respect, as he bowed deeply in Peg's direction. He then turned back to David. 'Please, sit down, Mr Castell. To what do I owe the honour of this visit?'

In David's opinion, the sudden display of respect

was overdone. But perhaps the fellow treated all guests that way, at least until he was sure that a donation to the institution was not forthcoming.

'Thank you,' he said, waiting until Peg was seated before taking the second chair in front of the desk. 'As to the reason for this visit, I am a reporter for the *Daily Standard.*'

'I see.' The room instantly chilled as the doctor measured his worth and found it wanting. 'If you think to come here and write a lurid story about your visit with the inmates, you are mistaken. Even Bedlam no longer allows such nonsense and we are far more strict than they ever were.'

'That was not my intention at all,' David assured him with a winning smile. 'I do not want to bother your residents. In fact, it is you we have come to see.'

'Me?' He supposed the doctor had reason to be surprised, since they had appeared on the doorstep unannounced.

'Indeed. You are possessor of some information that Lady Margaret and I would most like to have,' he said, giving the doctor another smile.

Dial looked between the two of them again, then focused on David. 'As I said before, the residents are not here to provide fodder for a London newspaper. I have promised their families privacy and they shall have it.'

'This is not concerning one of your current patients,' Peg interrupted. 'At least, I do not believe so. I am interested in learning more of certain enquiries my brother, the Duke of Scofield, made to you, concerning problems that we have been having with a mutual friend.'

Now the doctor looked worried. It was easy to reject the questions of a journalist from a minor London newspaper, but much harder to deal with the sister of a peer. 'I believe that His Grace intended that correspondence to be confidential,' he said, giving her a nervous look.

'Of course he did,' Peg said with a firm smile. 'But not from family.'

'If he had meant you to know, would he not have told you already?' the doctor asked, puzzled.

Peg gave him a pitying look. 'There are no secrets in our family. But Scofield is far too busy for me to be bothering him about this matter, nor is he the best one to be handling it. I know he wrote to you and I know that you recommended commitment. I simply need to know how much information he gave you to be sure his facts were accurate.'

'You doubt his understanding?' the doctor said, surprised.

'Now perhaps you can see why I cannot simply ask him about this,' Peg said with a conspiratorial smile. 'I am his favourite sister and am allowed some latitude. But one does not tell a duke that he might be wrong. Peers do not like to hear that.' Her expression softened and she gave the doctor a melting gaze. 'It would be most kind of you to set my mind at rest on the matter. Then neither one of us will have to bother Scofield with it.'

For a moment, the doctor's eyes glazed under the

weight of so much female charm. Then he replied, 'I suppose it would not be breaking a confidence to speak to a member of his family about it.'

'Of course not,' she said, beaming at him. 'Now just what did he tell you about the person that concerned him? He did not supply a name, did he?'

'Of course not,' the doctor said.

'That is good to know,' Peg said, placing her hand on her chest as if in relief. But knowing her as he did, David could see the faint flicker of irritation in her eyes that showed her disappointment that the matter could not have been settled simply with a single question.

She tried again. 'And how did he describe the symptoms of the person's malady?'

'Normal behaviour and even temper ninety-nine per cent of the time, but with rare cases of unexplainable, unprovoked murderous rage.'

'Unprovoked,' she repeated, giving David a significant look to remind him that all his searching for motive in the crimes was useless if they were dealing with an unpredictable madman.

The doctor nodded. 'He said she was totally normal one moment and the next—'

'She.' David could not help his explosive response.

'She,' Peg replied, with a smug smile, as if she had known it all along. 'Was there anything else he enquired about?'

'Mostly it was a worry that such madness might be passed to children,' the doctor replied. 'He was right to be concerned, for that is often the case.'

'And he wanted to know if there were any progressive treatments you could recommend,' she said to him.

'Unfortunately, there are not,' the doctor replied. 'Perhaps, if we had stopped the patient before she committed the first act, we might have saved her. But after the second?' He shrugged. 'One does not proscribe treatment for a mad dog or a man-eating tiger in India. The threatening animal must be eliminated permanently or caged. If the full weight of the law is not brought to bear on the lady he is worried about, then all I can recommend is permanent commitment.'

'And are there facilities for female patients?' she asked. The tremor in her voice hinted that she was afraid to hear the answer.

'We do not notice gender at such times as this. If the disease is the same, the treatment is the same,' the doctor said with a firm expression.

Peg nodded in feigned approval, but her eyes were wide with fear. Then she asked, 'Did you ever hear from my brother about a time or date for admission?'

'Unfortunately, no,' the doctor said. 'He informed me that he was not ready at this time to remand the lady into our care.'

Either he did not want to think of his lover in a place like this, or he had no authority to do anything. The powers of a duke were great, but not infinite. If the woman in question had family, it would be up to them to see to her care. Scofield could not snatch her off the street and lock her away for his father's murder without explaining all to someone and creating a scandal almost as great as the one everyone already believed about him.

'Well,' said David in a tone that implied he had heard all he needed to, 'does that clarify everything to your satisfaction, Lady Margaret?'

'I believe so,' she said, looking over her shoulder towards the main part of the building and shivering. David agreed with the sentiment, for it was a relief to know that they would not be able to visit the mysterious woman that Scofield had wanted to commit. As much as he wanted to know her identity, he did not have the heart to see the conditions of her imprisonment in a place like this.

After one last glance behind her, Peg rose, forcing the men to stand so they could end the interview.

'If there is anything more you need,' the doctor added, 'or any help restraining the patient...'

'We will come to you first,' Peg assured him. 'I am sure my brother was...satisfied with your answers and the facilities here seem most...comprehensive.' It was obvious the place horrified her, but it was also clear that this man was proud of the work he did and could not see the problems with it.

'We are also quite far from London,' the doctor reminded her. 'It is sometimes easier to keep problems distant from home, when one wishes to forget the tragedy of them.'

She shivered again and David tried not to think of what it would be like to be abandoned and forgotten in a madhouse, miles from friends and family. 'I understand,' she said, pulling her pelisse tighter around her as if fighting a chill. 'But now I think, Mr Castell, it is time we returned to the carriage to continue our journey.'

'Of course, my lady.' David laid a hand on her elbow and guided her back through the building to the front door as quickly as they could without seeming rude.

When they were concealed in the body of the carriage, he shouted the single word, 'Drive', and they were off. He added to her, 'I do not care where we are going, as long as it is away from here.'

She allowed herself another shudder. 'That poor woman. I do not care what she has done, I cannot imagine sending her to such a place as this.'

'Her,' David repeated in an amazed voice.

'A woman,' Peg said, smiling in relief. 'It was not my brother at all.'

'That is why he told me he did not care what I wrote,' David said thoughtfully. 'He is covering for someone else. But who?'

'Although Miss Devereaux might have the best motive for killing your friend, she was not Hugh's favourite when Father was killed,' she said. 'As I told you before, there was someone in the house with us the night Father died. It might have been her.'

'But what would motivate this woman to kill Sterling? The doctor did refer to two murders,' he said.

She shrugged. 'She might have been trying to protect Hugh. Or, if she is truly given to bouts of madness, she might strike with no reason at all. And if this is the woman whose lock of hair we found?' Peg sighed. 'I can see why it would render a marriage between them impossible. Even if he was willing to have a relationship with a murderess, he could not risk that his heir might grow up to be a madman.'

David scratched his head, bewildered. 'But we still have no idea who she might be. And I cannot ask the Duke for her identity, because if he feels we are too close to the answer, he might take the blame for the murders and we will never know.'

'I hope you do not press him,' she said. 'I am far too practical to think it romantic that he is willing to go to the gallows for love.'

'It would do me no good to force a confession from an innocent man.' David sighed. 'Especially since it would harm you and your family for no reason. Despite what you might think of me, I would not publish falsehoods just to spite your brother.'

She shook her head. 'I never suspected that of you. I know you only wanted justice for your friend.'

He nodded. 'I still want to know the truth of what happened to him. But I cannot see a way forward from here.'

'I suppose this means we will be returning to London,' she said. It was the sensible thing to do if their investigation was truly over. But now that the time was here, she did not want to be sensible. Knowing the strictures that awaited her at home, she wanted to keep running and never stop.

He ran a hand through his hair and cleared his

throat. 'We could do so, if that is where you wish to go.'

It was the last place in the world she wished to go if it meant that they would be parting. But if he did not want her, she could not demand that she be allowed to follow him to the ends of the earth.

'There is another option,' he said, looking up at her with a surprisingly nervous expression.

'Really?' she said, waiting.

He rubbed the back of his neck with his hand, staring at the ground for a moment as if gathering courage. Then he thrust his hand into his breast pocket and produced a simple gold ring. 'I am probably a fool for even asking this. I have very little to offer you but my love…' He paused, then started again. 'We are almost to Gretna. I can afford to keep a wife, of course, but not in the manner you are used to.'

It was the sensible thing to do, of course. If they returned to London to seek permission, Hugh would refuse him, just as he had Alister and Richard Sterling, and any other man who seemed interested in Olivia. If she truly wanted to marry David, this might be the only chance she had. So, trying not to be hurt by the awkwardness of his proposal, she replied, 'If it is a matter of convenience, we may as well continue on.'

He stared back at her, as if confused to find her response was as tepid as his proposal. 'Perhaps it seems to you that my feelings are not as truly engaged in daylight as they are at night. I assure you, that is not the case,' he insisted, wiping his brow with a hand-

kerchief and displaying a level of nervousness she
had never expected from him after the masterful way
he behaved when they were in bed. 'I love you and
want to marry you, and would have put this all much
more prettily had I taken the time to write it down.'

'You are a very good writer,' she agreed. 'It has
become my habit to read your articles in the *Daily
Standard.*'

'You have?' he said, momentarily distracted. Then
he shook his head. 'At least it is a way to prove to you
that I can make a respectable living. But if we return
to your brother and put the matter to him, I doubt he
will be as impressed as you. He will inform me that
you should not be marrying a man who works at all.
You are so far above me—'

'I am sitting at your side,' she reminded him, inch-
ing closer.

'And I agree with him. You deserve better,' he
said, but he did not move away. 'Not someone who
would trick you into running away with him, then
try to turn the trip into an elopement.'

If that had been his plan from the first she wished
he had been direct enough to tell her in the bookshop,
when her mind was not clouded by two more nights
in bed with him. But perhaps it was wise of him to
have waited. It had seemed easier to leave London
with him when the goal had been the adventure of
clearing her brother's name. If he had stated that his
only purpose was to cross the border and marry her,
would she have gone with him as easily? Or would

she have hesitated like Liv and Alister, waiting for permission that would never come?

What had happened was over and there was no telling if she'd have had the nerve. She could only know the answer that she was going to give him now. She stared into his face, trying to read his heart and asked, 'If you did not have to worry about the future or the past, what would you want?'

'To wake gazing into your eyes and to fall asleep with your kiss on my lips,' he said. 'To take my last breath with your hand in mine.'

It was what she wanted, as well. Now that he had found the words to describe his feelings, she wondered why she had ever doubted him. Her heart was beating so hard it felt as though it might burst if she took a breath to speak. She smiled through happy tears and managed to whisper, 'Take me to Gretna, my love.'

'Darling,' he said, reaching for her hand and slipping the ring on her finger. He took her in his arms to kiss her and for a time, all doubts were forgotten in the perfection of the moment.

Suddenly, the carriage jerked to a stop and they heard someone shout, 'Stand and deliver!'

In a single, smooth move, David released her from his kiss, pressed her back into the cushions and positioned his body in front of her to shield her from whoever might come. A moment later, the door opened and the barrel of a pistol poked in, gesturing him out of the way. 'Lady Margaret? We have come to bring you back to London before you do something you are likely to regret.'

Her brother's men had caught up to them, proving the foolishness of her earlier wish for a marriage with family approval. No matter what she might feel and how much he claimed to care, Hugh would never let her go. 'You needn't concern yourselves,' she said to the man at the door, knowing that arguing with an armed man was pointless. 'I am quite fine where I am, thank you.'

'Your brother begs to differ,' the man holding the pistol replied. 'We were told not to return without you, no matter what you claimed.'

That was it, then. There was no arguing with the Duke of Scofield, when he had made a decision. She reached for her reticule and prepared to get out of the carriage.

David pushed her gently back into her seat and continued to block the way, being foolishly brave in the face of a loaded weapon. 'Her brother sent you? A likely story,' he replied. 'I have no intention of handing a lady over to strange men on a public highway.'

The man holding the pistol sighed. 'Bring the maid.'

There was a moment's pause and Jenny's head appeared under the arm that held the pistol. 'Lady Margaret, I have a letter from your brother. He wants you to come home.'

'I bet he does,' David muttered under his breath.

'Move aside, Castell. It is only Lady Margaret

we want. The Duke was not overly concerned about what happened to you.'

And there was the rub. Her brother might not be a murderer now. But if she resisted his wishes, she might see her lover shot as a kidnapper. 'David,' she said, as gently as she could.

'Let me handle this, Peg,' he said, squaring his shoulders as the Duke's men took a menacing step closer.

But it was impossible to see how he would handle it. If she didn't do something, this was going to end with him dead or injured and her back in London, mourning his permanent loss. So she slipped the ring he had given her back into David's pocket, opened the door behind her and escaped her protector, dropping to the ground as David made a last wild grab to keep her near.

'Lady Margaret.' Her maid hurried around the carriage and engulfed her in a terrified hug and a shower of tears.

'Calm yourself, Jenny,' she said, pushing the girl away and forcing a handkerchief into her hands. 'Cease your weeping. I am fine and so are you.'

'And I am not,' David said, lunging for her again, only to be shoved back into the carriage by one of the guards. The other one was cutting the horses free of their harnesses to prevent pursuit.

'Discretion is the better part of valour,' she shouted to him as Jenny towed her towards another carriage, waiting to take her home.

'Shakespeare did not mean that seriously,' David shouted back, struggling with the man who held him.

'But I do. We will see each other again. In London. Somehow.' She was not sure that it was true, but she wanted to believe with a desire even stronger than the one that had kept faith for her brother alive. 'I love you,' she added, 'too much to see you hurt over this.'

David surrendered then and the last glance she got of his face before she was forced into the other carriage was a speculative look, as if he was already planning their next meeting. 'I love you, as well. I was wrong before. You will be safe with your brother. But I will not let him keep you now that you have promised to be mine.'

'We will have our day,' she agreed.

'Our life,' he corrected, freeing a hand to blow her a kiss.

The carriage door closed and she craned her neck out the window for one last look at him as the carriage started back for London.

Chapter Nineteen

By the time David returned to London, he'd had
ample time to come up with a plan to liberate his
beloved from the tyranny of her brother. But it disappointed him that he did not see much chance of
success in any of the ideas he'd had so far. He had
not expected the Duke to find them so quickly the
last time. If there had ever been an element of surprise to their elopement, it was gone now that she
had been dragged home from the road to Scotland.

It occurred to him that they might have better
luck if he did something completely unexpected and
acted like a gentleman. At the very least, it would remove any doubts from Peg and her brother as to the
seriousness of his intentions, if he made an effort to
get the Duke's permission before they ran off again.

So, the next day, he shaved close, put on his best
coat, and went to the front door of the Scofield town
house, announcing his desire to see the Duke.

He was, of course, refused.

In response, he waited outside, leaning against a tree on the opposite side of the street. The girls might be kept locked in the house, but the Duke could not remain inside for ever. When Scofield appeared, David hurried across to him, shouting, 'Your Grace, a moment of your time.'

The Duke gave him a look that was almost as deadly as the crimes David had recently accused him of. 'Castell. Why are you still here?'

'I have come to offer my apologies,' David said with his most winning smile. 'I have uncovered enough of the truth in regards to the murder of your father and my friend Dick Sterling. I know you are not guilty of either of them. I thought you would like to know that I will not be publishing anything about you or any members of your family.'

'I do not remember asking for your absolution,' the Duke replied, ready to push past him to get to his waiting carriage. 'And if you mean to apologise, you are guilty of crimes far worse than your pathetic scribblings.'

'You mean my trip north with Peg,' he said, smiling as the Duke flinched. 'I am sorry but I cannot apologise for that. I feel no regrets at all, other than that it was cut short before we'd reached our objective.'

'After two days on the road,' the Duke replied, giving him a look that consigned him to the lowest circle of hell.

David shrugged it off and continued. 'There is little that I can do to make Scotland come any closer. But there are many fine churches, right here in London. It might prevent an unfortunate delay in the future if you would do me the honour of granting me your sister's hand, so we might marry in the conventional way.'

At this, the Duke released an explosive laugh. 'Certainly not.' Then, he added, 'If and when my younger sister marries, she will be able to do far better than the likes of you.'

'And yet it is me she has chosen,' David said, still surprised at the fact. 'I am only asking for your permission because I am sure Peg would want me to consult you. Despite what it may seem, she respects your guidance and loves you quite outside of reason. You might like to know that her faith in your innocence never wavered, nor did her desire to follow me around, contradicting all I thought I knew until she had proved me wrong.'

What he had said was close enough to the truth. Even a girl as loyal as Peg had been to the Duke was to be allowed a few hiccups in her convictions. The information had the desired effect for he was sure that, for a moment at least, he saw the Duke's face soften into something closer to brotherly fondness. 'She is a good girl, for all the trouble she causes me.'

'And I can see why you want to keep her home,' David replied. 'But she is old enough to know her mind and decide her own future. I have offered and she has accepted. It only leaves your assent to make things proper.' When an answer did not immediately come, he added, 'We will be married, in any case. We are in love and meant to be together. But it would be better if you—'

The punch landed a moment after the words were out of his mouth. It was a single blow to the belly, probably delivered by one of the guards, since Scofield was still standing in front of him raising a hand to stop further violence. 'You already have my answer,' the Duke said in a soft voice. 'When you were last in my house, I told you to leave and not return. Do not make this more difficult than it needs to be.'

As David climbed to his knees, one of the guards was reaching for him, ready to strike him down again. But the Duke put a stop to it with another wave of his hand. 'Leave him. He is not worth the effort.' Then he continued his walk to the waiting coach and was gone.

When David was able to regain his wind and look up, he was embarrassed to see Peg looking out of one of the ground-floor windows. She had witnessed the whole exchange and was staring in horror, her hand over her mouth. It was not as he wanted her to see him, for he hardly looked like the gallant rescuer she needed him to be.

'No matter what His Grace has said, if you so much as wave, it will not go well for you,' said one of the guards before lifting him by the armpits and dragging him away from the house.

When they reached the end of the street, they set him on his feet and the second guard gave him a gentle shove to start him walking away. 'Goodbye, Mr Castell.'

'Au revoir,' he said, managing a smile before continuing on his way.

'Well, one good thing has come of this debacle,' Liv said, staring across the morning room at Peg.

'And what might that be?' she asked, glancing dejectedly out the window. She did not really want to see David again, if it meant seeing him manhandled by her brother's men and thrown from the property. But she could not seem to help looking for him.

'You are officially the black sheep of the family,' Liv said triumphantly. 'You were gone for days before they could find you and bring you back. That is far more daring than any of my brief liaisons with Alister.'

'I am glad to be of service,' Peg said with a sigh.

'Gone for days,' Liv repeated. 'Anything could have happened in that time.'

Could and did, Peg thought. It was too early to know whether she was going to miss her monthly courses. But if she did, she might finally have the leverage needed to force Hugh to allow a marriage. Though it was clear from the last unfortunate and very public meeting that he did not want to accept David's suit, there were some scandals that were impossible to hide. Surely it would be better to have a badly married pregnant sister than one that had not bothered to marry at all.

'Did anything happen?'

'What?' Peg's mind returned from the ether and she looked at her sister in surprise.

'Did something happen?' Liv said, glancing at the door to be sure no one was listening before leaning forward in her chair to hear the answer.

'Yes,' Peg said at last. There was no reason to keep a secret that everyone must have guessed anyway.

'Was it...nice?' her sister said, trying not to sound curious and failing. 'Did you like it?'

Now, it was Peg's turn to be surprised. 'You don't know? I thought, after all this time with Alister...'

Liv shook her head. 'We have never... But I do wonder...'

Peg smiled. 'It is very nice. It is quite wonderful, actually. But if Hugh will not allow us to marry, even after what we have done, I doubt I will ever do it again. What I did, I did for love and not some foolish quest for adventure.'

'You really want to marry Mr Castell,' Liv said, surprised.

'I would like nothing more in the world,' Peg said, glancing out the window again.

'He is not really our sort,' Liv reminded her, as if she had not already noticed the fact.

'It does not matter. I love him and he loves me.' She glanced at Liv again. 'You must understand. You love Alister, after all.'

There was a surprisingly long pause before Liv replied. 'Of course.'

'If you are not sure, then I recommend you wait for the physical aspects of love,' Peg said, feeling odd for offering advice to her older sister. 'I would never have done it, if I was not sure.' And even then, it had netted her nothing. She glanced at her sister and added, 'Do not forget that our brother is not forgiving of mistakes.'

It might have been unfair of her to say such a thing, for Hugh had been surprisingly gentle with her since her return. There had been no shouting or lectures. And, contrary to his earlier threats, he had not locked her on the wrong side of her bedroom door. He had merely sighed and announced that they would be leaving for the country in a few weeks, where there would be fewer distractions. It was hardly necessary. Since neither of the girls had been brave enough to attempt another shopping trip, it was more than quiet enough where they were.

Perhaps that was why the sound of Caesar barking in the backyard seemed so loud and frenzied. Whatever had set him off had him so unsettled that he could be heard all the way to the front of the house. The sisters glanced at each other, then hurried to the study window to see what had upset the dog.

'Do you think Mr Castell has come for you?' Liv whispered with a romantic sigh.

'If so, he is doing a very bad job of sneaking up on us,' Peg said. 'I do not see anyone there, in any case. Let us go to the kitchen door to get a better look.' When they did, there was still nothing out of the ordinary to see. But as the door opened, the dog shot between their feet and into the house, showing more life than he had in years.

'Come back here, you miserable beast,' Liv called, chasing him down the hall as frightened maids dodged clear of his crooked teeth like falling nine pins. 'Catch him,' she called to the footman by the front door.

Unfortunately for Liv, the boy had already met Caesar and stepped clear, opening the front door to allow him to escape. The pug disappeared through the opening and down the street as fast as his bandy legs would carry him.

'Get him!' shrieked Liv in a volume that roused the whole house and guards, front and back. 'Get him before he is run over by a carriage.' She raced out of the house after the dog, who had just taken a bite out of a passing under-butler before speeding across the street and into some bushes.

There was another, higher-pitched bark as a second pug crossed back in front of the house and Caesar reappeared, in pursuit and gaining, servants and guards following in an ever-increasing line.

'Dog fight,' Peg whispered in horror. 'Woe to that poor creature if Caesar gets hold of him.'

'Her,' said a quiet voice behind her. 'Her name is Cleopatra. If Caesar catches her, they will be occupied for some time and any gentlemen chasing will have to stop and shield the eyes of the maids.'

'And of my sister,' Peg said with a horrified grin, as she was jerked away from the front door and towards the back of the house. 'She had questions earlier about…'

'Let us talk as we walk,' David said, picking up

the pace. 'We do not know how long the lovebirds will be busy.'

'Can there be such a thing as canine lovebirds?' she said as they hurried out the kitchen door.

'In a month, maybe two, you may write home and ask,' he said, pointing to a carriage waiting beyond the garden gate. 'I suspect your sister will have two dogs by the end of the day and several more in a few months.' He hurried her the last few feet and into it, pausing only for a moment to say, 'I apologise for the brevity of this proposal, but, Lady Margaret, will you marry me?'

'Of course,' she said, hopping past him up into the carriage. He joined her and shut the door, signalling the driver so they could be on their way before they were missed.

'Where are we going?' she said, breathless.

'Gretna is north. So we are going south,' he said, smiling. 'And then, east. Or perhaps west. I have not decided.'

'You do not know?' she said, surprised.

'We will get to Gretna eventually,' he said with a serene smile. 'And we will be married, just as I promised, though you will be well and properly ruined before then. For quite some time we will navigate by flipping a coin if we do not want to see you dragged home again, as we did the last time.'

She stared at the coin in his hand. 'We might see all of England, before we get to Scotland.'

'Wales and Cornwall, as well,' he said. 'Let us see your brother's men follow that.'

She smiled. 'I have always wanted to travel.'

He smiled back and pulled the ring out of his pocket that he had been trying to give her on their last trip. 'Now, where were we when we were so rudely interrupted?'

She leaned into him, nestling herself under his arm as he took her hand, slipping the ring on her finger and holding it out so they could both admire it.

'You were telling me you wanted to hold my hand 'til your last breath,' she said, with a happy sigh.

'Which I hope is still quite distant,' he said, glancing out of the carriage window to be sure they were not being followed. When he was satisfied, he turned back to her, smiling. 'Although I am reasonably sure your brother is not a murderer, I do not want to give him incentive to change for the worse. When he realises you are gone, he will be angry.'

'But after several months without a sight of me, he will calm down again,' she replied, surprised to find that she did not really care.

'Coming away with me might mean permanent estrangement from your family,' he said, suddenly serious. 'But I will do everything in my power to make it right, once we are properly married.'

'It is not the sort of loss I feared when I thought you were going to write about them,' she said. 'That would have destroyed them. But this way, they will still be happy and healthy and out of the grip of the gallows. And, if I am honest, they do not need my help to be any of those things.' She smiled at the man next to her. 'I can live my life as I wish and I wish to live it with you.'

The arm that rested on her shoulder tightened to draw her even closer to his side. 'That is just what I hoped to hear.' He reached into his pocket for a coin. 'Let us see where chance takes us, my love.'

Epilogue

The house was too quiet now that Peg was gone from it. Liv had not noticed how much life her little sister brought to her days, until she had disappeared with David Castell. Despite Hugh's earlier threats, they had remained in the city, probably in hopes that Peg might return, with or without a husband.

Liv had heard nothing about either of them for six months, but she suspected it was not for want of trying on Peg's part. There had been letters, she was sure. But since Hugh had got into the habit of intercepting the post, she had seen nothing that he did not want her to see. She had contented herself with reading his cast-off copies of the *Daily Standard*, looking for articles by Mr Castell.

Surprisingly, the expected front-page article on her brother's crimes never appeared. Instead, Mr Castell wrote local news and travelogues from seemingly random locations. There were articles about Cornwall, Yorkshire, and most surprisingly, Italy.

Was Peg still with him? If so, the trip abroad might have been a honeymoon.

If there had been mail, Hugh would know the truth. It was reason enough for her to change her habits and rise early to breakfast with her brother. She had taken to avoiding him, after their father died, leaving the niceties to Peg who was unaffected by the scandal that surrounded them. But now that they were alone, if Liv did not learn to speak to him, she would have no one to talk to at all.

After years of polite silence, it was strange enough trying to make conversation with him, without doing it from the seat that her disowned little sister had traditionally occupied. She felt like an inferior replacement in what had been Hugh's rigid morning routine.

Today, she looked over at him and the carefully guarded stack of letters beside his plate. She smiled, helping herself to a cup of chocolate, and asked in the most casual way possible, 'Is there anything interesting in the mail?'

The sound of a human voice seemed to startle her brother almost more than the question did. He looked up at her as if he had forgotten she was there. Then he replied, 'No. Nothing of interest.'

'Nothing from Peg?' she added, hoping to catch him off guard.

'We do not speak of your sister,' he said, hurriedly picking up another letter.

'There are many things in this house we do not speak of,' Liv said. 'I guess I will have to add her to the list.' In her final weeks at home, Peg had done little more than force them to talk about things that were better off kept secret. Liv wondered what she had found. Perhaps she had written of it in some of the letters that Hugh would not allow her to have. 'And why do we not speak of her?' Liv added, not really expecting an answer.

Hugh busied himself with his coffee, pretending he had not heard.

'Has she murdered someone, as well?' Liv added, to provoke him.

This got a response. Hugh twitched with such violence that his coffee slopped into the saucer. Very deliberately, he put the cup down and replied, 'That is a question you would have to ask her.'

'But I doubt you will allow me to,' Liv countered. 'I assume she has been banned from the house.'

'She is welcome here, if she returns alone, and can prove to me that she will behave like a virtuous lady, so I do not have to fear pollution of your character by her presence,' Hugh said with a sigh.

'Pollution?' Liv scoffed. 'Until recently, I was far more trouble than she ever was.'

'I am aware of that,' Hugh said without looking up. 'But the situation has changed. Since it appears she has married that wastrel Castell, I do not hold out much hope of her return.'

'Married?' Liv said with a triumphant sigh. It meant that her escape from the house had been successful. It made the increased surveillance of her comings and goings almost worthwhile.

'An elopement to Scotland,' her brother allowed. 'If you can call that a wedding. My agents chased the pair of them around half of Britain before they actually tied the knot.'

'If you hadn't tried to stop them, they'd have been married earlier,' she could not help reminding him.

He grunted in response. 'So Castell told me when last we spoke. And now, apparently, she is with child. Attempting to gain an annulment will be even more scandalous than their marriage.'

'Is she requesting an annulment?' Liv said, staring at her brother.

'No.' He made another sound of disgust. 'In her correspondence, she proclaims herself blissfully happy.' His expression changed to one of confusion. 'And Castell has not asked me for a settlement, as I expected he would.'

Liv adopted an expression of mock surprise. 'Why, that means that you have absolutely no control over what Peg does.' She smiled and sipped her chocolate.

'But you are still here,' he said, with an equally mocking smile.

'For the time being,' she agreed, reaching for a muffin. Hugh might think he had her sewn up properly, unable to get away. But it was only a matter of time before Alister came up with a plan. Then they would run away to Scotland, just as her sister had. Hugh would be left alone in the house to repent for his sins and remember the days when he had loyal sisters to keep him company.

The day was coming when she would be free. And it could not come soon enough.

* * * * *

If you enjoyed this book, why not check out these other great reads by Christine Merrill

The Brooding Duke of Danforth

"Their Mistletoe Reunion" in
Snowbound Surrender

Vows to Save Her Reputation

*And look out for the next book in the
Secrets of the Duke's Family miniseries,
coming soon!*